The Amish Girl

Samantha Jillian Bayarr

A note from the Author:

While this novel is set against the backdrop of an Amish community, the characters and the names of the community are fictional. There is no intended resemblance between the characters in this book or the setting, and any real members of any Amish or Mennonite community. As with any work of fiction, I've taken license in some areas of research as a means of creating the necessary circumstances for my characters and setting. It is completely impossible to be accurate in details and descriptions, since every community differs, and such a setting would destroy the fictional quality of entertainment this book serves to present. Any inaccuracies in the Amish and Mennonite lifestyles portrayed in this book are completely due to fictional license. Please keep in mind that this book is meant for fictional, entertainment purposes only, and is not written as a text book on the Amish.

Happy Reading

Chapter 1

Ten-year-old Amelia bolted upright in bed, her heart racing from the crack of lightning that split the air on such a quiet, summer night. The crickets' song had suddenly stopped, and all she could hear was the muffled sound of her own heart beating.

Tilting her head to listen, her eyes bulged in the dark room as she tried to focus. The pale moonlight filtered in through the thin curtains beside her bed, a gentle breeze fluttering the sheers against the sill. Outside her window, the cornstalks in the field swayed, flapping their leaves with a familiar rhythm.

It smelled like rain was on the way.

She sucked in a ragged breath, her exhale catching as if she was out of air. Her heart beat faster still, fear flowing through her veins like ice water. A bead of sweat ran down her back between her shoulder blades, causing her to shiver.

Had she been dreaming?

Scooting to the edge of the bed, her legs felt a little wobbly as she let her feet down easy against the cool, wood floor. It was a comfort on such a warm night, though it increased her risk of wetting her pants.

She reached for the door handle, but pulled her hand away, the hair on the back of her neck prickling a warning. Tip-toeing back to her bed, she climbed in under the quilt, crossing her legs and leaning on her haunches to keep from wetting herself.

An unfamiliar voice carried from the other room, causing her heart to race and her limbs to tremble. It was an angry voice.

Another shot rent the air. It was the same noise that had woken her.

Her mother cried out, calling her father's name.

"*Mamm,*" Amelia whispered into the night air.

Once again, she pushed back the light quilt, her need to see her mother forcing her wobbly legs to support her tiny frame. Moving slowly, she made sure to be quiet, cringing every time the floor planks creaked.

It was unlike her parents to be so loud in the middle of the night, but something was terribly wrong.

Wondering who belonged to the mysterious voice, she listened to him arguing with her mother. Her voice was shaky, like she was crying, and it frightened Amelia.

"We don't have any money," her mother cried. "Please don't do this!"

Where was her father, and where had the other man come from? Who was this man, and why was he upsetting her mother? She peeked around the corner from the hallway, spotting a man dressed in black, with a gun raised and pointed at her mother.

Amelia shook, and her teeth chattered uncontrollably.

A single lantern flickered from the table, her eyes darted around the dimly-lit room, trying to place her father. She pulled in another ragged breath when she spotted him lying on the floor, blood pooling around his head. The noise that had woken her hadn't been in her dreams, it was the gunshot that had killed her father.

Every instinct in her warned her to hide, but her feet seemed unwilling to take her back to her room.

"This is your last chance," the gunman warned. "If you won't give me my money, you lose your life!"

"No!" she screamed. "Please, I don't have it."

"I had to spend the last ten years in jail for nothing," the man said through gritted teeth. "While the two of you spent *my* money on this nice farmhouse, and all those acres you have out there? You've been enjoying your life all these years with your horses and chickens and such, while I've been locked away with nothing!"

He aimed the gun at her, and she dropped to the floor, crying and pleading with him to spare her life.

He ignored her pleas.

Amelia shook violently, her gasp masked by a second gunshot, killing her mother right before her eyes.

She let out a strangled cry, and the man holding the gun turned toward her, his eyes locking with hers for a moment.

"Well, now, isn't this a nice surprise!" he said, tilting his head back and laughing madly.

His laugh sent chills through her, causing her bladder to empty uncontrollably.

For a moment, Amelia was paralyzed with fear, her feet unmovable in the puddle of urine. Lightning lit up the room, a crash of thunder bringing her back to her senses.

She forced her feet to propel her forward, heaving them as if they were chained to the floor. Swinging open the back door, she ran toward the cornfield that separated them from the Yoder farm. Glancing over her shoulder, she looked back to see the man was behind her, hobbling as if he had a lame leg.

"Don't run, little Amish girl," he called after her. "I'm not going to hurt you!"

She entered the cornfield, visualizing the path she took on a daily basis when she visited with Caleb, her neighbor and friend. She'd never come through it in the dark, and her mind was too cluttered with fear that ripped at her gut to follow the path. Bile rose in her throat, but she swallowed it down as she ran. Cornstalks whipped at her face and arms, her mind barely aware of the stings that meant they'd drawn blood.

She stumbled, her breath heaving, as she scrambled on her hands and knees long enough to right herself. Her bare feet painfully dug into the rocks and dirt in the field, but her instinct was to stay alive.

The small barn at the back edge of the Yoder property had been a meeting place for her and Caleb. A place where they'd played with the barn cats and their kittens, and washed their horses after a long ride. But most of all, it was a place she knew there was a gun. Caleb had taught her how to shoot it, using tin cans for practice, but she'd never thought to turn it on a human—until now.

The main house was still too far away. Amelia knew her only chance of surviving this man's fury was to surprise him with the unexpected. All she wanted was for him to leave her alone, and she didn't have the physical strength to run any further. Pointing a gun at him the way he'd pointed it at her mother was the only thing on her mind. It drove her to reach the barn before the man who intended to kill her.

All she could think about, as she ran faster than she'd ever run before, was getting her hands on the gun she knew was in the Yoder's barn. The gun would give her power—the power to stop this man from killing her. Neither her *mamm* nor her *daed* had a gun, and now they were dead—both of them. Amelia didn't want to die. It was one of her biggest fears in her short life, and right now, that fear drove her to stay alive at all cost.

She entered the barn out of breath, her eyes struggling to focus. If not for the large window near the tack room filtering in the flashes of lightning, she would not be able to find her way. Crawling under the workbench, Amelia grabbed for the strongbox that housed the gun. The lock on it had long-since been broken, but she shook so much, she struggled to pry open the rusted lid. A flicker of lightning revealed the Derringer inside the metal box, and she snatched it quickly, and cracked the barrel forward. She'd done it a hundred times before when she and Caleb practiced, not knowing she'd ever have to use it to defend herself.

Shoving her shaky hand inside the box of ammunition, she grabbed haphazardly, and then loaded two bullets. Gripping the small handgun, she aimed it toward the door, waiting for her stalker.

"Come out, come out, little Amish girl. I'm not going to hurt you," the man called out to her.

Amelia sucked in a breath and drew the loaded gun out in front of her, darting it back and forth until her eyes focused on her assailant. Lightning blinked him in and out of her sight.

She flinched when he struck a match and lit the lantern hanging up just inside the doorway, turning up the flame until it lit up the room.

Amelia stayed crouched down under the work bench in the tack room, gun extended in front of her. She held her breath when she saw the look in his eyes, and knew he meant to do her harm.

The man spotted Amelia's feet underneath the work bench and smiled widely, but it wasn't a kind smile. "Why are you pointing a gun at me?" he asked. "I'm not going to hurt you!"

Her entire body tensed up, fear making her grip on the gun grow tighter. She stared at him, breathing hard through clenched teeth, her hands shaky.

He laughed at her. "We both know you aren't going to shoot me."

She pulled back the hammer of the gun fast and sure, without taking her eyes off of him.

His hands went up in mock defense, but he laughed nervously. "This isn't funny, Amish girl. I put my gun away, but you better put that gun down before I have to hurt you!"

She raised the gun as he moved slowly toward her, keeping it trained on his heart. Though she only meant to intimidate him the way he was doing to her, she had no intention of pulling the trigger. Her aim was too accurate.

"Put the gun down, little Amish girl," he said through gritted teeth.

Thunder rumbled, making her jump as he lurched toward her.

She let out a scream as she accidentally squeezed the trigger, a single shot discharging with a puff of smoke from the end of the barrel. Her eyes closed against the explosion that rang in her ears like the crack of thunder from the oncoming storm. When the smoke cleared, she could see that the bullet had gone straight through the man's chest, and he'd collapsed to the ground in front of her.

She kept the gun trained on him, staring into his unblinking eyes; her hands shaking and her breath catching, as she strangled the whimpering that intermittently escaped her lips.

She hadn't meant to shoot him; hadn't meant to kill him, but now he was dead—just like her parents.

Chapter 2

Amelia woke up gasping.

She'd had the dream again.

Beads of sweat rolled down her back between her shoulder blades, her breath heaving as she shook off the bad memory.

She stretched her weary arms and yawned, remembering that today was different.

Today was the day she was going home.

She wiped away bittersweet tears from her eyes, looking at the alarm clock she'd punched the snooze button on more than once. She sprang from the bed, knowing if she was late for her last session with Sister Agnes, she would not be leaving today. The nun had warned her that her final evaluation was required by the state in order for them to release her, and if they thought in any way she wasn't ready, she would remain at Fenwick Hall for another six months, until she would be eligible for another evaluation.

Everything was dependent on the answers she would give the psychiatric nun today, and those answers, carefully calculated, stood between her and freedom from the cold halls of the institution.

She swiped at the snarls in her long, brown hair with a brush, and then twisted it to a perfect bun at the nape of her neck. Picking up the prayer *kapp* she hadn't worn since she'd first arrived at the state-run facility, she pinned it to her head as a symbol that connected her to her past. It had yellowed with age, and was a bit too small, but she suddenly felt lost without it. Almost as if today had transported her back to the life she'd left behind when she'd become a part of the *English* world.

She readied herself in the light brown dress she'd recently sewn, removing the old prayer *kapp,* and replacing it with the new *kapp* she'd also made in preparation for her return to the Amish community. She would return to her home, whether she was shunned or not. It was the only home she had.

She studied her reflection in the mirror as she contemplated the day she'd almost been dreading for the past eight years. Her intention was not to deceive the nuns with conniving answers today, but to gain passage to the long-awaited freedom she'd dreamed of.

She knew she wasn't ready to trade the safety of the orphanage for the home she prayed she'd never have to return to, but she feared if she didn't leave now, she might never go. Not because she didn't miss her home; she simply wasn't ready to face the ghosts that would likely haunt her for the rest of her days. She would never forget the sound of the gunshots that had brought death that night, nor the smell of gunpowder she could still sense if she closed her eyes even for a moment. It had made for many a sleepless night, lending itself to the sort of insomnia that brought night-terrors at the slightest drift of her eyes.

Amelia straightened her smock apron, and hurried down the hall toward Sister Agnes's office. Holding up a hand to knock, she paused, took a deep breath to calm her nerves, and then whispered a quick prayer for courage.

She'd rehearsed what she'd say, and the casual way she would carry herself during the evaluation, but nothing could have prepared her for this meeting. Not really.

If her *Mamm* was here, she'd tell her to stiffen up her bottom lip and do chores to work through her troubles, reminding her that there wasn't anything that couldn't be worked out while busying herself with some *gut,* hard work. But *mamm* wasn't here to tell her, and it just wasn't the same as being able to hide her smile when her *mamm* would look at her firmly and warn her about what the Bible said regarding idle hands.

Her hands had been nothing but idle for the last eight years, and *Mamm* had been right. It had given her too much time to think. Too much time to worry—about what today meant.

"Come in," Sister Agnes welcomed her with a smile. "I've been expecting you."

She pointed to a chair in front of her desk, and Amelia reluctantly sat. She crossed her ankles, tucking her feet under the chair. She knew it would help to keep her restless legs from her usual bouncing when she'd come for her usual sessions. She was determined to appear calm, and remain still throughout the meeting, even if it meant she had to run up and down the fire escape afterward in order to expel the nervous energy she already felt creeping up on her.

Sister Agnes put a hand to her chin and tilted her head. "How long have we been meeting, Amelia?"

Is this a trick question?

She'd been a ward of the state for the eight years since her parents were killed. For eight years since she'd accidentally taken the life of Bruce Albee after witnessing him heartlessly shoot her parents.

"Eight years," she answered quietly, trying her best to hide her annoyance.

Sister Agnes nodded politely. "Do you believe you're ready to put what happened behind you, and start your new life?"

What kind of question is that?

She'd relived that night every day for the last eight years, and no amount of therapy had removed the memory the way she'd hoped. She'd volunteered to help with the younger children at the orphanage to keep her mind busy, but it hurt her so much when they'd get adopted and she would have to tell them goodbye. After the first few times, she'd hardened her heart, not allowing herself to become attached to her young charges. The work helped to keep her mind occupied, and if not for that, she worried she might have gone mad from all the worrying.

Amelia nodded. "I believe I am."

"How do you feel about leaving here and being on your own without your family?"

"I'm ready," she said, trying to convince herself more than Sister Agnes.

The nightmares about that night had recently returned, and no matter how many times Sister Agnes tried to comfort her, nothing could remove the fear she still felt in the very pit of her soul. The nuns had tried their best to encourage her to feel at ease about returning home, but only dread filled her. Granted, she was happy to be leaving the orphanage, but with nowhere else to go but back to the very place that caused her gut to sour, she couldn't help but feel scared and alone.

"Do you know why we couldn't place you with another family?" the nun asked.

She shrugged, truly having no idea why.

When she'd first arrived at the orphanage, she'd wondered if being placed with a nice family might ease the pain of losing her parents, until she'd seen the notes in her chart that read *not eligible for adoption.*

She hadn't meant to see the notes, but Sister Agnes had been called out of her office shortly after her initial intake, and had left the file open on her desk when she'd left Amelia alone in there for nearly half an hour. There were times over the years when she wished she hadn't been so curious that day as to read her file, because before then, she'd had some sort of hope for adoption, even if it was only false hope.

"Our intention is always to place our young ones with families that best match them, and we had gotten a letter from the Bishop in your community that went into great detail of regret as to why no family there would be permitted to adopt you."

Amelia sat up straight, giving Sister Agnes her full attention. "What did it say?"

The nun lowered her gaze. "It said you'd been shunned."

"I'm not surprised."

"What will you do without the support of your community once you leave here?"

Another shrug.

The community had turned their backs on her— shunned her for taking the life of the murderer. It hadn't mattered to them that it had been self-defense. She'd been raised to live at peace with her fellow man, and violence was looked upon as unacceptable, no matter what the circumstance. Having a gun, in their eyes, was a mortal sin, and to use it in violence—even self-defense, was unforgivable.

To the community, Amelia's sin now caused her to fit into the world, and she was shunned to take her place among the rest of the sinners. There would be no tolerance for her, and no acceptance for what she'd done. After the news circulated about the murders, the fear spread even faster, and they'd put her under the ban.

No one from the community had even attended her parents' funerals.

She would never forget the cold way that Bishop Graber had treated her during the brief, and obligatory service for her parents. It was the last thing he would do for them, and she knew, even at that young age, that he hadn't wanted to. *Frau* Graber had tried to offer her comforting words when they'd approached the state-owned vehicle she was locked in, but Bishop Graber had given her a look of disapproval. Amelia hadn't even been permitted to leave the car that had driven her to the institution. Afterward, the Bishop and his wife had left her parents' graveside, and the car had taken her away. They hadn't even given her a chance to say goodbye, let alone to mourn the loss. She'd cried quietly in the back seat of the vehicle, alone and afraid of her future.

No, they would not likely be welcoming her back into their midst. Bishop Graber was a strict man, and would not tolerate Amelia's return to the community. He'd strictly forbidden the members to take her in after her parents were killed. Because of the shunning, she'd been placed in the hands of legal authorities, who, in turn, handed her over to the orphanage.

As the years passed, she'd come to realize that it was fear that had made them turn her away, but Bruce Albee was gone, and there was no reason for them to fear her, though they might beg to differ.

In the eyes of the community, she was no different than the man she'd shot.

Surely, not even a public confession would spare her from remaining under the ban.

She was determined not to let that get in the way of her returning home.

"I suppose I'll manage the same way anyone else does when they leave home to go out into the world on their own. Mrs. Winters at the bakery, gave me a *gut*—good recommendation to her cousin, Mrs. Miles, who runs the bakery back in Pigeon Hollow. She gave me a week to get myself settled, and then to go see her for a job there. With the new job, I believe I will get along alright."

Sister Agnes smiled.

"It sounds as if you have a sound plan for your future, but how do you feel about what you did—the shooting? And how do you think it will make you feel to return to a place that brought you such sorrow? Are you ready to face all of that?"

Truth be told, Amelia wasn't sorry for defending herself, because to do so, would mean she was meant to die along with her parents. She did, however, feel a very deep remorse for taking the life of the man, regardless of his murderous acts. He'd intended to kill her that night, and for that reason alone, she could not regret what she'd done. She'd struggled with the guilt and the remorse, but only for taking his life. For eight long years, she'd lived with what had happened. The fact that it was an accident had not made it any easier on her conscience.

"I wish I could take it back, but it's something I'll have to live with for the rest of my life. I know what I did was wrong—in the moral sense, even if it seemed right at the time. I believe there are reasons it can be right—self-defense, for example, and I know the difference between right and wrong. I didn't shoot that man on purpose. It was an accident, but I accept full responsibility. As for returning to my home, I do have some apprehension, but I think that's unavoidable. I suppose I won't know how I *really* feel until I get there."

They'd had many a long talk about responsibility and acceptance, and Amelia knew it was the answer the nun was looking for.

Her nod would confirm it.

"Since your home was paid in full at the time of your parents' death, I don't worry about you keeping a roof over your head," she began. "You've proven you're capable of supporting yourself by holding down a job for the past two years. The only thing that concerns me is the condition of the home. It may not be livable in its current condition. What will you do to remedy that?"

 She sighed, wondering what had become of her home since she'd been gone.

"With the money I've saved from my job at the bakery, I should be able to get some supplies if I need them. I attended a few barn-raisings when I was younger, and I'm certain I can still remember how to swing a hammer the way my *daed* taught me. He used to say I was the boy he never had!"

"It sounds as if you've got everything figured out," Sister Agnes said. "You know we'll help you until you turn twenty-one, so if you find you're unable to adjust out there, you're always welcome to come back."

"I'll be fine," she said nervously.

Truth was, she was unsure of how she would manage anything about being in the house she grew up in and all the memories—good and bad, that came along with it. She had dreamt of returning home all these years, and had not been back there since the night Bruce Albee had chased her out. She wasn't sure how it would feel to return to the home where the man took her parents' lives, but she longed to be able to call anywhere *home*.

Amelia stood up and looked out of the office window, noting how befitting it was that the grey sky matched her mood. Shaking off the stress that consumed her at the moment, she tucked away the bad memories in the back of her mind, praying they'd stay there. She was determined not to suffer an anxiety attack today.

This was the day she would go from being a scared little girl, to a brave grownup for the first time since the night that turned her life upside down.

Every detail of that night was etched in her mind, and though she missed her home, she hoped her return would not interfere with her ability to heal from the grief of losing her parents. That grief had weighed her down, and kept her from living her life. And although she would never stop missing her parents, she was ready to let go of the sadness and try to live a happy life; if for no other reason than it was too exhausting to hold onto the sadness any longer.

With so many changes coming her way, she hoped she would not fail at it and have to return to Fenwick Hall.

Her family home was rumored to have been boarded up and neglected after the removal of her parents' bodies, and the evidence had been collected by authorities to close the case. She had no idea the true condition she'd find the home in, but it was all she had left of her childhood—before that dreaded night that had changed everything.

Now, she was determined to face every bit of it, despite her fear that nothing would ever be the same again.

Chapter 3

Amelia stood in front of her childhood home, unable to move. The taxi that had brought her had long-since gone, the driver leaving her few belongings at her feet before taking off. He'd talked her ear off about the history of the house as if she didn't know, and tried to pry details about that night out of her before they reached the home. She'd kept quiet the entire time, not answering him, and though she hadn't wanted to be rude, she just couldn't talk about it with the stranger. She figured he probably thought she was a little bit looney, but she often felt that her silence about that night was the only thing she had left of her sanity.

She stood in the yard, barely able to see over the tall
grass and weeds that swayed in the wind as if
sending whispers from the dead. Storm clouds
pushed their way overhead, threatening to release
their fury on the dilapidated home. The oak tree
where her tire swing hung had overgrown, draping
angry branches over the width of the house, the rope
frayed, and the old tire cracked and misshapen.

Lightning flickered across the dark sky, causing
Amelia to flinch. The rumble of thunder rolled
across the thick air, rattling the broken glass in the
weathered and sun-bleached window panes.
Cracked and peeling paint lent to the unkempt
facade of the neglected home.

She perceived from the exterior, that the house was
not inhabitable, just as Sister Agnes had warned, but
Amelia had nowhere else to go. She looked at the
set of keys in her hand and scoffed at the door that
was half-open and falling away from its hinges.
Leaves and muck piled up at the entrance, and she
wondered just how long the door had been left open.
Several boards still remained across the doorway,
blocking her view of the inside of the home, and she
imagined someone had kicked the door open—a

thief, maybe, and crawled under the boards that were meant to keep such a person out. A stray board or two hung haphazardly from the windows, but had also been torn away.

Lightning cracked, and thunder roared, announcing the coming storm. She raised her gaze toward the house, shaking off the hazy memory of that night. She'd worked hard to hide the details of it in the back of her mind and close them away, but they had suddenly rushed back as if it was yesterday.

Shuddering against gusts of wind, large raindrops pelted her with an angry force, but she remained unmoved. Uncontrollable sobs consumed her as she collapsed on her haunches, crying louder with every crack of thunder.

Lord, how can I stay here after what happened? I've begged you for courage, but I don't feel it. Bless me with the courage I need to overcome my fears about this place. Send your comforting arms to help me feel safe.

Warm arms wrapped around her, picking her up with a strength only a man could have. He cradled her against the contours of his chest and brought her to the shelter of the covered porch. She continued to sob, barely aware that she'd been moved, as he set her safely onto the weathered porch swing.

I remember this swing.

Many a warm night, she and her childhood friend, Caleb, would catch fireflies in the yard, while her parents watched from the solace of the swing, swaying lazily in the summer heat.

She was faintly aware of the man rushing back out into the rain and grabbing her bags, and setting them down at her feet. He removed his black, felt hat—an Amish hat, and poured the water from the large brim.

Amelia lifted her gaze to meet the man who'd pulled her out of the rain. "Who are you?" she asked soberly.

Kneeling in front of her, he pushed back wet strands of hair from her face and smiled. "It's me, Caleb."

Her breath hitched as she put a hand to his chest as if needing to touch him to make him real. "You can't be," she said, searching his blue eyes. "Caleb is just a *boy!*"

She held out her hand at the measure of his height as if he was a young boy, and Caleb clenched it, bringing it back to his cheek. His eyes drifted closed for a moment before looking at her again.

"I *was* just a boy the last time you saw me," he said gently. "But now I'm a man. I've grown up—just like you, Amelia."

He was right. His lanky arms and legs had grown longer and filled in with muscle, and his broad shoulders were strong, like a man who'd seen many days of hard work on a farm. His jawline boasted a day's growth of light whiskers that matched his thick, blonde hair.

Her lower lip quivered as she peered into his familiar blue eyes. "You did grow up, didn't you?"

She collapsed against his sturdy frame and sobbed, but these tears were happy ones. He pulled her into his arms, kissing her forehead and shushing her.

"I've waited so long for you!" he whispered to her. "I was so afraid I'd never see you again after…" he let his voice trail off, not willing to finish the sentence, but they both knew what he couldn't say.

"I've missed you too," she said with a hiccup. "I can't believe you're here!"

"When I heard you were coming back, I couldn't wait to see you."

"How did you know I was coming back?" she asked.

"The community talks a lot," he said. "And even though I'm no longer part of it, my cousins still talk to me."

"But how do they know?"

"Bishop Graber wrote to the home where you were and asked to be notified when you'd be returning. They sent a letter a few days ago."

"Why aren't you part of the community?"

"Because of what happened," he started to say.

"Because of what I did," she interrupted him. "I'm so sorry."

"It isn't all your fault," he admitted. "I'm the one who taught you how to shoot the gun. The Bishop wouldn't listen to me when I told them my *daed* had nothing to do with it—that you and I had found the old gun in the barn, but they told him he should have had more control over me, so we were shunned."

"I'm sorry," she said, looking at him. "But why do you still dress as Amish if you're not part of the community?"

He flipped the strings on her prayer *kapp* and smiled. "I could ask you the same thing.

She forced a weak smile. "I suppose I don't know any other way."

He leaned back and pulled her tiny frame back against him. "I suppose I don't either."

The rain had calmed a little, the storm moving away from them, but with Caleb here holding her, she felt the safest she'd felt in a long time.

After a few minutes, he moved to the swing beside her, tucking his arm around her. She rested her head on his shoulder and pushed gently with her foot, setting the swing into motion. The chains squeaked more than they had when she was young, but it was a soothing sound. She missed her parents, and the feeling of home.

Looking up toward the door, she wondered if she'd be able to walk through it with Caleb here.

She shivered, and he pulled her close, but it didn't help; they were both soaking wet.

"Let's get you inside and I'll build a fire so we can get warmed up."

She took in a deep breath and blew it out slowly. "I suppose I have to go in sometime, don't I?"

He grabbed her hand. "I'll be right there with you, and I'll stay as long as you want me to."

She squeezed his hand, thinking he shouldn't have offered such a thing, because she might never want him to leave. He'd certainly grown up very handsome. She imagined they'd likely be ready to marry this season if they'd not been apart all these years. The thought made her blush unexpectedly, and she was glad it was getting too dark for him to notice.

Caleb stood up, his eyes scanning the overgrown landscape. "I'm sorry about the condition the place is in. Every time I thought about coming over and taking care of the grass or the house, I just couldn't bring myself to come here—until now."

"I don't expect you to do this—it's my house, and I've got a lot of work ahead of me, but I think I can make it work. That is, if I can work up the nerve to go inside."

He smiled. "Don't worry. I'll help you get this place looking brand new again."

With her hand tucked safely in Caleb's, she braved her way toward the front door, and then stopped, the boards across the doorway a welcome hindrance.

He let her hand drop. "Stand back and I'll see if I can't get rid of these boards."

Ducking under the slats of wood, he stood inside the doorway and kicked the boards. Each one fell with a crack that made Amelia jump, despite the fact she expected the noise. It seemed lately, every little noise seemed to magnify and put her teeth on edge.

He stepped back out to the porch and smiled nervously, trying to make light of the situation before she saw the terrible condition of the interior of the house.

"This kind of reminds me of the tree house we tried to build in that dead tree in the field, and the branch fell after I hoisted the bundle of wood to build the base. I sprained both my wrists bracing myself for that fall, and had both my arms in a sling. Remember?" He chuckled. "I remember feeling pretty special that you had to feed me lunch every day at school and help me with my school-work. I left those slings on for three extra days after the doc told me I could take them off—just so you'd keep helping me."

Amelia struggled to put the memories together, but didn't remember things the same way he'd described. She had blocked out a lot of her childhood, thanks to the years of therapy she had been through that forced her to consistently remember all the bad things. She'd spent the last eight years reliving the tragic events, and she'd not had time to remember the good things in her life, and so they'd slowly left her.

"I'm sorry, but my memory isn't so *gut* these days."

Caleb's shoulders fell and he became a little confused. He and Amelia were such good friends as children, until the tragedy happened, and she was forced into a state-run facility with no family or friends to see her through any of it. He had been waiting for the day she'd return and he could be reunited with his friend. How could she not remember such an important thing about him?

Caleb smiled weakly and shrugged; he didn't want to overwhelm her by saying too much, but he was determined to help her remember the good things she had forgotten from her childhood, even if it would take some time.

Her gaze fell. "I'm afraid of a lot of things now, and I don't know why. I don't remember enough of the *gut* things, but please—tell me as many of the *gut* stories as you can, so I'll have them to hang onto. Perhaps then, I'll be able to get rid of the ghosts of the past, and maybe, just maybe, my nightmares will go away too."

"I'm ready anytime you are," he said.

"I'm afraid," she said soberly, holding back on his hand. "I can't seem to bring myself to go inside just yet."

Caleb couldn't blame her for that; he'd begged his *daed* to burn down their barn after seeing the deceased gunman in there. Having to clean up the blood had almost convinced his father to go ahead and burn it down, but since he'd been shunned for having the gun that had killed Bruce Albee, there would be no one to help him rebuild—no barn-raising would be offered to them.

"I'll help you in any way I can."

Amelia smiled. Somehow, hearing Caleb offer to be there, even if he did seem to be a stranger to her, made her feel more at home. "I'd like that."

Amelia looked up at the home where her family was once together and happy, feeling a little less sad, and maybe even a little hopeful. She felt a little unsure about the repairs needed to make this place livable again, but with Caleb's help and friendship, she felt a sense of peace about being home.

Chapter 4

Amelia stood frozen in the doorway of her childhood home, clenching Caleb's hand as if she was falling, and he was the only thing that stood between her and sudden death.

"You're going to be fine," he assured her. "I'm going to stay right here with you."

She finally worked up the courage to take a step forward through the door. The last bit of daylight filtering in from the back windows highlighted the dust in the air. The paint on the walls had faded to a color that made Amelia's stomach turn. Except for the sound of the rain hitting the tin roof, the house was eerily quiet—like a tomb.

All the furniture was gone except her *mamm's* rocking chair near the fireplace. In her mind's eye, she could see her *mamm* rocking gently by the warm fire while mending—she was always sewing something. A new dress for Amelia, or quilt squares—anything to keep her hands from being idle.

She stumbled over the rubble that used to be her life, as she made her way to the dirty chair. She'd never been allowed to sit in it, but she lowered herself into it now. It felt foreign, and not at all comforting the way she thought it might. It hadn't brought her close to her *mamm,* and in fact, gave her a chill. She rose to her feet and looked at the chair. It was just a chair, but it represented her deep loss. Her *mamm* was gone, but the chair remained as if to be a place-holder to fill in the gap where her *mamm* used to be.

She looked around at the disheveled room that had been ransacked. Thieves had most likely broken in and taken it all, and she was thankful they hadn't set the home ablaze. She hoped that perhaps they had left something behind; anything, that Amelia could hold onto. Perhaps beneath the rubble, she could find some semblance of her childhood, but right now, all she could see was filth and chaos.

She walked across the room, the wood floors creaking beneath her feet. Her breath hitched, and tears pooled in her eyes at the site of the bloodstain that still discolored the rug—the place where her parents had been killed.

She slowly walked around the bloodstain to the kitchen, where she and her mother had spent so much time baking and preparing meals. A few broken dishes cluttered the counters, food staples had been torn open, most likely from critters foraging for a morsel.

She stood at the kitchen window above the dirty sink, the view of the outside making her heart ache just as much as the inside did. It made her sad that so many years had gone by, and no one had given her childhood home the attention she felt it deserved. It was in a total state of disrepair. It wasn't just the cracked windows, or peeling and chipped paint; it was dirty, and no one had cleaned the rug.

Why hadn't anyone cleaned the rug?

Amelia could hear the crackle of fire from the other room, the strong aroma of black locust logs mixed with the slightest hint of hickory and oak filled the stale air. With that mixture of woods, it would burn longer and hotter, removing the chill from the damp, autumn air.

Noises from the other room made her shiver. She knew exactly what was going on, without even turning around to look.

Caleb had rolled up the rug and was dragging it out of the house.

Relief washed over her, while a lump formed in her throat, making it difficult to breathe. It wasn't that she wanted to keep the rug, but removing it meant removing all trace of her parents. It needed to be done, and logic told her to remain in the kitchen until the deed was done.

When she heard movement in the front room again, she turned around to be certain it was Caleb.

It was.

She let out the breath she'd held in, folding her arms across her torso and rubbing her arms to get them warm. Her teeth chattered, and she wondered if it was safe to go back into the front room so she could stand near the fireplace and warm herself. She worried that Caleb may still be trying to spare her the evidence of death that still remained in the home. Her memories alone could not be erased of that night, and no amount of cleaning or removal of rugs would strike it from her thoughts.

Though Caleb helped calm her anxieties, she still worried that coming back to her childhood home may not have been the best thing for her mental health. She was determined to begin her life anew, but the ghosts of the past had a way of creeping into her thoughts constantly. For the past eight years, she had been labeled the little Amish girl who'd shot and killed a man, and now was the time to break free from that. She was neither Amish nor *English;* neither a daughter, nor a friend. But perhaps some of that could be changed. She had longed to be home for eight long years, but this was not how she'd envisioned it.

She stood at the kitchen window watching for a moment as Caleb tightened the hinges on the front door and tested the lock.

He turned to her as she entered the room. "It closes and locks, and even though the windows are cracked, none are broken. I can tape them, or board them up, but if I board them up, you won't get any sunlight in through them."

She took in a deep breath and exhaled slowly, not ready to make any decisions, no matter how trivial. "Do what you think is best."

"If it were me, I'd tape them until we can replace the glass."

She nodded, and lowered herself to the brick hearth, extending her hands toward the warmth of the crackling fire. She stared into the flames, her vision blurring and her mind drifting backward.

"This is your last chance," he said. "Give me the money, or you lose your life!"

"No!" she screamed. "Please, I don't have it."

Caleb brought in a fresh bundle of firewood and dropped one of the logs.

Amelia jumped up and screamed, her breath heaving, a hand to her chest as if she was suffering a heart attack. She paused for a moment as she realized that the noise had come from the log hitting the floor, and not a gunshot. She began to cry, and Caleb set the remaining logs on the hearth and pulled her into his arms, allowing her to sob.

"I'm so sorry," he said, stroking her hair. "I didn't mean to startle you. I'll be more careful not to make any loud or sudden noises. I should have known you would still be in shock just being here."

"I know it was an accident," she said with a sniffle. "But maybe it was a bad idea to come here. I'm as scared as a jack-rabbit. I can't stay here by myself. I'll end up scaring myself to death before the light of dawn."

"I doubt that," he tried comforting her. "You're a lot braver than you think. I'm not sure I could stay here alone either after what happened, and I'm a grown man now."

"I have a few dollars saved aside for making repairs, but I suppose I'll have to find a place to stay in town until I've gotten used to being on my own. Maybe then I can return."

"Or," he said excitedly. "You can stay in my room, and I'll stay in the *dawdi haus*. I'll help you fix this place up, and you can stay with me in the meantime."

"What about your *daed?* Shouldn't you ask him if he minds?"

Caleb didn't answer right away.

"I don't have to stay with you if it's going to cause trouble."

Caleb cleared his throat. "That's not the problem. He hasn't been the same because of all this, it's been really tough on him."

"I'm so sorry, Caleb," she said with a sniffle.

"With the death of my *mamm* the year before, he didn't have time to recover before being shunned. It was just too much for my *daed,* and he's not been the same since."

"I feel responsible; I'm so sorry," she sobbed.

"It isn't your fault. I'm two years older than you are; I should have known better than to teach you to shoot that gun. I only did it because I had a crush on you."

Amelia gently pulled away from him to look him in the eye. "You did?"

"*Jah,*" he said. "I loved you because you were the best friend I've ever had, but I had a crush on you, too."

"You were the best friend I've ever had too," she said in response.

He looked at her, searching for more.

She smiled. "I had a crush on you too!"

He pushed her still-wet hair off her cheek. "I'll always love you, and you're still my best friend. So, I won't take no for an answer; you're staying with me until we can get this place in shape."

She loved him still, too, but she just couldn't bring herself to say it. Those feelings scared her. She'd loved her parents, and they were gone. She couldn't take another loss if something were to happen to Caleb.

"What about your *daed?*"

"I've been taking care of him since I was twelve years old. He isn't going to know you're there."

She looked around at the puddles of water from the leaking roof, the dirt and leaves that had blown inside and covered the floor, and had to admit she didn't want to stay here. There was no furniture, no dishes, and she hadn't brought any cleaners with her. Even if she had, it would take her at least a few days of cleaning to make this place partially livable. Not to mention, she hadn't dared to look in her room to see if her bed was still there, and even if it was, she was certain it would be unusable, and likely need to be thrown out to the road for the refuse truck. Between not having a place to sleep, and the ghosts not quite cleared from her home, she'd be foolish not to accept his hospitality.

She smiled. "You talked me into it."

Chapter 5

Caleb showed Amelia to his room, snatching up a few dirty things from the floor out of embarrassment.

"Sorry about the mess," he said shyly. "I got dressed in a hurry this morning."

She tried to hide her snicker, not wanting to embarrass him, but she thought it was cute the way he scrambled to get his personal things so she wouldn't see them. She'd already noticed that the rest of the house was not as tidy as it would be if there was a woman in the house. She thought, perhaps, she could clean a little in the morning when she woke to surprise Caleb and his father with some breakfast.

They'd had a small meal that Caleb had already prepared. They'd warmed it up when they'd gotten back from her house, and Amelia had found it awkward sitting across from Mr. Yoder at the dinner table. He hadn't even spoken to either of them. He'd looked up at Amelia a couple of times, but he hadn't said a word. His eyes were sad and aged, not at all like she remembered him. He and Caleb had always been so close, and they'd done everything together. Amelia vaguely remembered his mother, and didn't want to mention her, knowing it was probably still just as painful for him as her own loss had been for her.

His dad mostly stared off into space, and Caleb had not exaggerated when he'd told her that he completely cared for him. She'd offered to wash the dishes after dinner, but Caleb had urged her to leave them until morning. They were both exhausted, and would have a long few days ahead of them to get her house in order before she had to start her new job at the bakery with her new boss, Mrs. Miles. She was grateful she'd already had an opportunity to meet with her briefly about the position when she'd gone for a visit with her cousin at the bakery near the orphanage, but she was most grateful the woman understood her need to remain employed, as there would be no help for her from the community.

It was still storming, and Amelia was grateful she would not have to sleep in her home all alone. Thunderstorms still frightened her, because of the terrible storm the night her parents were killed.

She flinched each time lightning flickered throughout the dark room, and shuddered at even the most subtle rumbling of thunder, jumping whenever it would shake the house with a deafening force. She pulled the quilt around her tightly, wondering if she would ever be able to get through a storm without being scared. Aside from the heavy drumming of rain against the tin roof, and the steady wind scraping tree branches against the siding, the house was quiet.

She was used to hearing babies crying and children whispering throughout the night, and the soft footfalls of the nuns as they walked the corridors of Fenwick Hall. To be without those familiar noises that she'd grown used to over the past eight years, she feared she would not get any sleep. Tucking the quilt in around her shoulders, and resting her head on Caleb's pillow, she turned her face toward the soft fabric that smelled just like him; a musky mixture of his natural scent, mixed with horses and hay. She stuffed her face deep into his pillow, and breathed in fully with her eyes closed, thinking she could get used to that manly aroma. If not for circumstances that had torn them apart, she imagined she and Caleb might be well on their way to being married. Being away for so many years, had left a gap in her heart, but being with him now in his home, and in his bed, only brought a desire for him she didn't know was there—until now.

Before long, Amelia drifted off into a deep sleep, her heart feeling light, and bordering in-love.

A crack of thunder startled her, but she couldn't move. She tried to wake herself, but she just couldn't move her limbs. It was as if she was paralyzed. Her lashes fluttered as lightning flickered, lighting up the room in little snippets. The figure of a man stood in the doorway of the room, but she still could not move.

She tried to scream, but no sound escaped her lips.

Another crack of thunder brought the man to life. Chills ran cold down her spine, her limbs helpless to save her from certain danger.

Again, she tried to scream, but could not find her voice.

The man took a step into the room, lightning flickering behind his large figure, preventing her from seeing his face. She groaned, trying to flee from the threat of peril.

"I'm not going to hurt you," the man's voice said.

A shrill cry let loose from her throat as she bolted upright in the bed.

Sucking in air, she lifted her eyes toward the door where the man was, but he was not there. The door was closed, and the storm had passed.

She'd only been dreaming.

Wiping the sweat from her cheeks, she jumped when a hasty knock sounded against the door.

"Amelia!" Caleb shouted from the other side of the door. "Are you alright?"

Bone-weary, she climbed out from beneath the warm quilts and went to the door.

He opened the door before waiting for her to answer. "I'm sorry to intrude, but I heard you screaming from downstairs. I came in to put more wood on the fire, and I was worried you might be hurt."

She pushed her way into his arms, her limbs shaky. "I'm sorry, I was dreaming—about the night I shot *him.*"

Footfalls from the hall padded angrily across the wood floor. Mr. Yoder tightened a plain, brown robe around his waist, and glared at Amelia.

"What are you doing in my house?" he barked. "You've brought nothing but trouble to the community—you, and your folks, when they helped rob that bank when they were on their *rumspringa.*"

Amelia's breath hitched, tears pooling in her eyes.

"*Daed,* you don't know what you're saying," Caleb said. "We don't know that they had anything to do with the robbery."

"How else did they know the man?" he questioned
Amelia. "I'll tell you how; they're just as guilty of
robbing that bank as the man that went to prison for
it. That's why he came after them and shot them; for
spending all that money on that broken-down farm
they left you with!"

She started sobbing, Caleb holding onto her with the
arm he'd kept around her waist.

"You shot that man with a gun you found in my
barn," Mr. Yoder continued. "Bishop Graber didn't
believe me when I told him I had no idea about the
gun. I blame *you* for the Bishop putting me under
the ban, and I don't want you in my house."

"She was just a child when that happened," Caleb
defended her. "That was eight years ago, and you
should have forgiven her a long time ago instead of
holding onto all the bitterness that's eaten you up all
these years."

"I have forgiven you," he said, turning to Amelia.
"But that doesn't mean I want you in my house. Get
out!"

Amelia ran back into Caleb's room and scrambled
to get her things, uncontrollable sobs clogging her

throat. She stuffed her clothes in her bags, not wanting to give the man any more chance to sling insults at her.

"Go back to bed, *Daed,*" Caleb said firmly to his father. "I'll handle this."

"Get her out of my house!" he shouted as he stomped back to his room.

Caleb entered his room, and rushed to Amelia's side. He stopped her hasty packing and pulled her into his arms, stroking her hair and whispering calming words to quiet her sobs.

"He doesn't know what he's saying, Amelia," he said. "Don't pay any attention to him."

"Is that what everyone thinks? That my parents were guilty of robbery? No wonder I was shunned!"

"It doesn't matter what other people think," he reassured her. "All that matters is what *you* think."

She sniffled, leaning against his sturdy frame, burying her face in his robe. She breathed in deeply, remembering his scent from his pillow. It was a comforting smell—like *home.*

"If I was to be honest with myself," she said. "I'd have to admit I've had my doubts about the whole thing. When Sister Agnes told me I was inheriting the house and the land, and that it was all paid for, it made me wonder, but no one wants to believe their parents are capable of committing a crime. The only thing that gives me confidence is that my *mamm* died because she told the man she didn't know where the money was. She wouldn't have said that if she could have told him where it was. He might have spared her life if she'd been able to hand him over the money. My parents were not thieves, and they didn't buy my house and land with stolen money. The property isn't worth much. The amount that was stolen was more than five times what the house and acres are worth. Surely, they would have lived more extravagant lives if they had all that money. Instead, they struggled, and my *mamm* made quilts and sold them to help keep up our bills. They just weren't bank robbers. It's too horrible to even think about."

"I believe you," he said gently. "And I believe in your parents' innocence."

"*Danki,* that means a lot to me. I don't know what I'd do without your friendship right now."

"You're never going to have to find out," he said, kissing her forehead.

Tipping her head upward, she searched his eyes, finding what she was looking for as he pressed his lips softly against hers.

Chapter 6

The sun was beginning to make its way across the horizon, the joyful song of chirpy birds waking her. She opened her eyes to greet the morning, but struggled for a moment to remember where she was.

The *dawdi haus* at the Yoder farm.

Caleb had switched places with her, moving back into the main house, and back to his room, while letting her have the small house in back. After his father's reaction to her being in the house, she figured it was best to steer clear of him. Instead of going into the main house to do last night's dishes as she'd planned, she figured it was best to stay in the *dawdi haus,* and perhaps get a little bit of breakfast there, and then move on to her own house. She wouldn't burden Caleb anymore by staying here if she didn't have to. She intended to work hard to get the place cleaned enough that it would be livable.

Slipping into her work dress, Amelia headed to the small kitchen to put together some sort of breakfast. She was terribly hungry, and figured it might be the end of the day before she'd get another meal.

She was grateful to find some fresh buttermilk biscuits and honey. Caleb's honey was the finest in the county. He'd always kept his hives in a clover field, which gave it a very mild and sweet taste compared to wildflower honey.

Amelia walked over to her house from the road, avoiding the path through the cornfield. She felt she'd rather walk all the way down the long drive, and all the way around the property in order to get over to her house, rather than taking the shortcut through the cornfield that still scared her just to look at it. She walked briskly past the field of corn, trying hard to block out the screams from her parents that seemed to drift over the rippling cornstalks as they fluttered in the breeze. Stepping on a twig, the snap from it startled her as if it was a gunshot. Would she ever be able to get past the fear from that night? That cornfield was the reason she'd become an insomniac. Just hearing the leaves rustling sent shivers down the back of her neck, raising the hairs at her nape.

Perhaps selling the house and the land would relieve her of all the ghosts from the past. As she came upon her house, she thought it looked different in the light of day. Though the day was overcast, it had been almost too dark yesterday to see the house fully when she'd been dropped off, and she hadn't realized just how bad the house was, until now.

Caleb was already there, working on the outside of the house. She was so grateful that he was as dedicated as she was about getting her home back to the same *homey* state she remembered it being. Growing up in this home always felt safe for Amelia, it may not have been much, but her parents had made it the best they could. She was especially looking forward to getting the kitchen in order, where she and her mother spent so much time together.

She could already see that Caleb was busy in the back, cutting the tall grass with a sickle. It was going to take a lot more work than trimming down the overgrown landscaping to get this place an order. She looked at the sagging roof, wondering how it hadn't collapsed by now with the weight of the tree branches leaning on it, and a small section of the tin roof had blown off over time.

The shutters hung on only by a hinge, the windows all cracked, and the paint peeled and chipped over most of the wood siding. It all disappointed her. When she was a young girl, her *daed* had kept the home up quite nicely. Her *mamm* had flowers around the front, and a potted plant on each end of the porch. Her mother had loved flowers.

Caleb spotted her, and leaned the sickle against the side of the house. Swiping his black hat from his head, he wiped his brow with the back of his shirtsleeve.

"It's a little warmer out here than it was yesterday," he said. "I could've sworn winter was on its way with the rain we had yesterday, but it looks like it's going to rain again today. We should get to work on the roof if you're ready, we can go into town and get some supplies to fix the holes."

She was eager to get inside and get to work cleaning, but she also relished the idea of going into town with Caleb. At this point, any type of distraction to get her mind off of having to go into the house and face the ghosts of her past, she was up for. The way the house looked now in its condition, was nothing short of a haunted house. But only it was haunted by her past and tragedies she herself had witnessed.

Caleb helped Amelia into his buggy, enjoying the warmth of her hand as he assisted her. He placed his other hand at the small of her back as he helped her up, without thinking anything of it, as if it was the most natural thing in the world.

He settled in beside her, wondering if he should be so forward with her. He'd known her all his life, and loved her just as long, but the gap in time since he'd last seen her had made them strangers, hadn't it? He didn't think it had, but he thought, perhaps, she might, and scooted slightly away from her, leaving an inch or so between them—for propriety's sake.

Amelia tucked her arm in Caleb's, moving in closer to him, and leaned her head on his shoulder. She knew he'd put a measure of distance between them with an uncertainty of her feelings. She knew him all too well. She also knew that even though they were no longer part of the community, those who saw them together would draw a conclusion about them keeping company, and would surely gossip about it.

He smiled and leaned his head against hers for a moment, and then set the horse in motion down the road. His heart felt light, as if the weight of the past eight years had lifted from him. The years of anticipation and wonder about her.

As they drove through the sleepy town of Pigeon Hollow, Amelia noted how many things she recognized. Things had not changed as much as she'd feared they would have, but the atmosphere was certainly not the same. No longer did neighbors send up a hand to wave to them, as they had when she'd gone for drives with her parents. There had always been a sense of support from the community, and she had no idea that being shunned would feel like this.

Caleb felt Amelia become rigid next to him, and knew she was feeling the tense stares from neighbors. "Don't pay them any mind," he said, trying to comfort her. "They're only wondering if it's really you! They'll get over it in a few days and stop staring so much. In the meantime, don't let them rattle you. They're only curious. They don't mean you any ill-will."

"It feels like it from where I'm sitting," she said. "I'm sure they don't want me here because of what happened."

"When they remember you were only a child when that happened, and you've grown up, things will be different. They're just afraid, that's all."

Amelia looked him in the eye. "Afraid of *me?*"

"Nee—no! They're afraid you'll bring back the dead with you—and trouble. They're afraid of history repeating itself."

"How do you know this?" she demanded. "And how can history repeat itself, when the man who killed my parents is also dead and buried?"

He turned the horse down Main Street, toward the lumber yard. "It can't, and it won't. But that doesn't stop their wild imaginations from running away from them. It's human nature. My cousins tell me things, but sometimes they exaggerate, so who knows what's true and what's not?"

She sighed heavily. "Being back here isn't exactly a picnic for me either!"

"Don't worry about it," he said. "It's all in the past. The talk will die down eventually."

He pulled the buggy into the parking lot of the lumber yard, and hopped down to tie up the horse. Then, he helped Amelia out of the buggy, trying his best to be a gentleman. He knew this *buggy ride* didn't count as courting—they were merely going into town for supplies, but prayed it would count for something more than friendship. He'd wanted to marry her since he was ten years old, and now that they were old enough, it almost felt that too much time had passed and it was too late. He prayed it wasn't so, but that would depend on her.

She looped her arm in his, leading him toward the garden area. "Look at all the pretty flowers! I wish I had the money to plant some. Remember all the flowers my *mamm* used to have out front of the *haus?* I miss that."

"I remember your *mamm* getting after me because our goat got loose and trampled most of her flower patch, and ate the rest of it. That goat ate everything in sight, so *daed* unloaded him on his cousin, and they unloaded him on an *Englisher* who tried to bring him back!"

"I barely remember that. Seems I've blocked out a lot of the good because of the bad."

"I'll help you remember only the *gut* things."

She forced a smile, feeling uneasy about his promise. Funny thing about memories—they just weren't the same for everyone.

Chapter 7

Caleb climbed into the buggy next to Amelia, warmth radiating from her. He couldn't believe how exciting it was to be near her, and he had barely slept all night from thinking of her. Now, he'd spent almost the entire day with her, picking out supplies to fix her house up. He'd missed her so much, and hadn't realized just how much until he'd seen her yesterday. Was it possible for the two of them to pick up where they'd left off so many years ago? He realized they were only kids then, but his love for her was just as real then as it was now.

"When we get back, I'll have just enough time to clear a path before the sun sets. I'm eager to get that roof fixed before more damage is done to the inside of the house."

Amelia looked up at the sky, the storm clouds rolling in made her shiver. "Since they won't be dropping off the supplies until the morning, what are we going to do about the roof now?" she asked. "Do you have any more buckets at your house to catch the leaks coming inside?"

"I'm certain I can find a few in the barn," he said, looking up at the sky.

Amelia pulled her shawl around her, shivering and praying the weather would hold out until they got back to her house. As they passed the cornfield, wind picked up and rustled the leaves.

I won't hurt you, little Amish girl, a voice echoed over the tops of the cornstalks.

Amelia's breath hitched. "Did you hear that?" She cried.

Caleb patted her hand. "What am I listening for?" He asked.

"You didn't hear that voice—that eerie voice when the wind blew?"

He shook his head, and it brought tears to her eyes.

He hated to see her cry. He always did.

When they were young, he was there to comfort her when her parakeet had flown away. She'd cried then too, but it was nothing compared to when her parents had died. She'd been there for him when his *mamm* had passed, but his *daed* had not let him cry then. He'd cried later, and she'd held his hand, just as he'd done for her then, and now was no different. If she claimed she heard something, he would believe her. He knew even if it wasn't real, it was real to her, and for that, he would comfort through whatever troubles she encountered. It was tough enough for her to be here under normal circumstances, but to live in fear, things were going to be harder on her than he suspected.

"Don't let your imagination run away with you," he said, giving her hand a little squeeze. "I'm right here with you, and no one is going to hurt you."

Amelia felt embarrassed, thinking to herself that she was hearing things that weren't there. She hoped

Caleb would not think her to be a little crazy. But she was beginning to wonder herself.

As they pulled into the yard, Amelia let out a shrill scream.

Caleb steered the horse away from the house, and away from the red splatters and splotches that covered the front door and a portion of the porch.

He hopped out of the buggy to examine just exactly what it was. When he came upon it, he realized it was blood, just as he'd suspected. He couldn't help but wonder who would do such a thing. That much blood could only come from something large. He prayed it had come from an animal that had been slaughtered, and not from a human. His heart sped up and he shook at the site of it. Amelia started to get out of the buggy, but Caleb waved a hand at her, urging her back in.

"Let me check things out here first," he whispered loudly. "Then, if it's safe, you can come in."

"I want to leave," Amelia cried.

Caleb went back toward the porch and listened, but the wind howled, thunder cracked, and lightning flickered across the gray sky. He crept up onto the porch and tried the front door, but it was locked. He walked around the perimeter of the house, checking the back door and all the windows. They appeared to be secure.

When he returned to the front of the house, Amelia was sobbing so hard her shoulders were shaking. He hopped up into the buggy and pulled her into his arms.

"We can leave if you want to," he said. "But it doesn't appear as though anyone was in the house. It looks to me like blood from an animal, and I didn't find anything other than the blood. I can hose it off in no time, so we can get back to work on the house."

"I don't think I want to stay here," she said, shaking. "I'm scared."

Caleb smoothed her hair, cradling her head against his shoulder. "I'm sure it was just a harmless prank from some of the *English* kids around here. They can be a little cruel."

"You call this a harmless prank?" She cried.

He hadn't meant to belittle her worries, but he wasn't about to fall apart with her. One of them had to keep their head, and he was determined to be strong for her.

"I only meant that there are a lot of farms in this county, and a lot of them slaughter their own livestock. I have no reason to believe that it's human blood. If you're that worried, we can always call the sheriff. But I honestly think it's a one-time prank, and there isn't any cause to get the sheriff involved."

"You don't think we should call the sheriff's department now?" She cried. "This isn't a normal prank. Eggs smashed against the house, and toilet paper in the trees are pranks, and this is definitely more serious than that. I think this was meant to scare me away."

"That's possible," Caleb admitted. "But you have to be strong and let them know that you're standing your ground. I think it was done because they are afraid of *you!*"

"I don't want people to be afraid of me," she cried. "I only want to live in peace; to be left alone, so I can move on with my life. I've been so stuck in the past, I'd like to move past it all, and I can't do that if I'm going to be persecuted."

"Let me get this mess cleaned up, and we'll forget it ever happened."

"Until the next time!" she cried. "What if the next thing they do gets someone hurt?"

"I already told you, I'm not going to let that happen."

He hopped back down from the buggy, leaving her there crying and shaking, while he unraveled the hose and sprayed off the porch and the door. Whoever had done the deed had obviously done it shortly after they'd left, because it was mostly dried, and it did not come up easily.

Amelia sniffled, watching the bloody water drain down the porch steps and onto the grass. It sickened her to see it, in the same way the blood stain on the living room rug had sickened her. But just as the rug, Caleb was removing it from her sight.

When he finished, she climbed down from the
buggy, her legs wobbly, and her teeth chattering—
not from the cold, but from fear.

Chapter 8

Taking in a deep breath to steady her nerves, Amelia boldly tucked her arm in the crook of Caleb's elbow, and allowed him to assist her up the steps of the porch.

"I'm a grown up now," she said, giving herself a pep-talk. "No matter how bad this is, I can own up to it and stand my ground."

"*Das gut,*" he encouraged her. "Keep telling yourself that."

She didn't imagine she'd ever be able to sleep here alone—unless Caleb proposed, and since she didn't expect him to any time soon, if ever, it looked as though she'd be spending a lot of sleepless nights here. There were too many things she couldn't push from her mind, too many ghosts that continued to haunt her. And now, it seemed, that someone was determined to make things worse for her. She wanted to believe Caleb; that it was only a harmless prank, but the sight of blood made her ill down to the very pit of her stomach. If someone was indeed trying to scare her away, they were doing a fine job of it by throwing blood on her house.

Now, standing on the porch, she stopped, unintentionally digging her fingernails into Caleb's bicep. "I can't do this!" she cried. "I can't go in there. I won't!"

Caleb's heart clenched behind his chest wall, fearing he may break down. He could not force her to go in. He would not. It was cruel, to say the least. "I'll be right here with you whatever you decide. But if you can't even go inside, you might want to consider putting the place up for sale."

"But then I won't have anywhere to live and I'll *really* have to start over again," she complained.

Caleb smiled. "I can think of somewhere for you to live. A place you've already made yourself comfortable in."

Amelia became rigid next to him. "Oh, no! That's only temporary, and *only* as long as your *daed* doesn't find out I'm there. Staying in your *dawdi haus* is almost as bad as staying here—no offense!"

He chuckled lightly. "I don't take offense to that. It hasn't been easy for *me* to live with my *daed* since all this happened. I can only imagine how much worse it might make you feel."

"If I had a *dawdi haus* I'd let you stay there—so you could get away from all that tension, I mean," she said to him.

"*Jah,* I do," he said, putting his arm around her waist. "What's it going to be? Are we going in, or are you coming back with me and staying in the *dawdi haus?* Either way I look at it, you're hiding from something—my *daed,* or the past."

She took another deep breath, hoping it would calm her nerves, but she still shook just as much. "I've already been in there, and maybe it wasn't as bad as I thought. I just got shaken up from the blood, but I think if I don't face this, I'll always be running from something, and that's no way to live."

"You're right. Let's get in there and clean the place up. I'm sure that will make you feel better about being here."

She nodded and allowed Caleb to lead her up to the house. He turned the key and opened the door, the creaking setting her nerves on edge.

Noticing her jumpiness at every little noise, he tightened his grip on her. "I'll oil the hinges so it's quiet."

She nodded, walking robotically beside him. Once inside, her gaze traveled over the dim room, feeling panic rising up from her gut. Her breaths quickened, her nails digging into Caleb's arm again. She cringed, unable to quiet the voices from that night.

Constant cracks of thunder and flickering lightning did not help ease her fears about this place. Her breaths came quicker and the walls seemed to be closing in on her; tunnel vision made it hard for her to see, and she feared she may pass out.

"Take me back," she cried. "Take me back to your house. I'd rather face your father and all his judgment than the ghosts of this house."

"You're right Amelia," he said, calming her. "Perhaps tomorrow if it's not storming, maybe then we'll be able to get through this. I think the storm is bringing back too many bad memories, and maybe you're just not ready for all of that yet."

He cradled her in his arms, as he led her out the door and into his buggy. He would take her back to his home where she could feel safer, and he would not let any harm come to her no matter what.

Caleb clicked to Chestnut, urging the horse to do his bidding. The gelding knew the way home, but Caleb could see that the weather had even put him on edge. Amelia leaned her head against his shoulder the entire way back to his house, and he felt bad for pushing her too soon.

"We'll get an early start tomorrow; you'll see when they drop off the supplies in the morning. It'll be a fresh, new day, and we'll get that place in order so there won't be any trace of the past left in your home. Unless it's something you want to be there."

"That sounds good to me," she sobbed.

They drove up to the yard, and he pulled around quietly to the back and let her off at the *dawdi haus,* and then drove the buggy a few feet to the barn so he could pull the buggy in for the night. He was trying to be discreet so that his father would not know that she was there. It wasn't that he was trying to be sneaky, he just didn't want any trouble for her.

As he began to unharness Chestnut from the buggy, he heard Amelia screaming from the *dawdi haus* without a pause. He ran to her as fast as he could, frightened that someone was hurting her. Out of breath, he shouldered his way through the door, finding Amelia screaming at a blood stain covering the rug in the front room of the tiny home. The stain was almost identical to the one he'd found on the rug he'd rolled up and disposed of from her own home.

The only difference was, the blood was fresh.

Who would've done such a thing?

"Go into the bedroom," he ordered her. "I'll roll up this carpet and get it out of here."

She shook her head. "No! What if he's in there?"

"What if *who* is in there?" Caleb asked.

"The murderer!" she said in between sobbing.

"There is no murderer, Amelia," he said calmly. "He's been gone for eight years! This is just a prank, I'm telling you."

"Don't you think we should get the sheriff's department to tell us what they think?" she begged.

"Let me think about this for a minute," he said as he walked into the bedroom to check to make sure that everything was secure. When he was certain she was safe, he went out to the living room and made quick work of moving the sofa aside, and the two chairs and coffee table. Then he bent down to roll up the rug.

"I told you to get that girl out of my *haus*," his dad's voice thundered from the front door.

Caleb looked up at his angry father, who was dressed in rubber boots, his rubber apron, and he was covered in blood. It was what he wore when slaughtering one of the livestock, and it was apparent he'd just been to slaughter.

Caleb leered at his father. "Did you do this?"

"Do what? I've been busy most of the day getting two pigs ready for the smokehouse."

Caleb sniffed the air and realized his father was telling the truth about that much of it, but he'd avoided answering him. "Someone soiled this rug with blood. It's still wet, and this stain is too large for it to be a simple explanation!"

The man scowled, his gaze traveling to the rug beneath his son's feet. "What happened here?" he asked. "Did the Amish girl do this?"

"No!" Caleb said, befuddled at his father's statement. "I was just asking you the same thing. Someone splattered fresh blood all over her front door and her porch today, and now we come back here, and there's blood on this rug, and we have no idea who did it. And for the record; she's no more Amish than you and I are!"

"I warned you not to let her stay here," he said. "I told you she would bring nothing but trouble and *death* to this house. Get her out of here; I won't tell you again!"

The man turned on his heels without answering his son, leaving Caleb filled with fear and panic. Was his father capable of such a thing? Would he go to such lengths just to scare Amelia away? One thing was certain; he would have to discourage Amelia from calling the Sheriff's Department because he wasn't about to call the law on his own father—that is, if he did this.

He prayed it wasn't so.

Chapter 9

"I can't stay here alone!" Amelia said. "I need someone to stand guard. I'm already such a wreck, I don't think I'll be able to sleep otherwise."

She was still shaking, and he hated seeing her like that.

Caleb let out a heavy sigh. He didn't blame her for not wanting to be alone. Admittedly, he didn't like the idea of her being alone any more than she did. "I can stay on the sofa, but only until you fall asleep, and then I'll have to go," he offered. "I really shouldn't stay in the same house without an escort, but I think this situation could be considered an emergency of sorts. If my *daed* found out, he'd take me out back of the barn for a *talk* for sure and for certain!"

"I'm sorry to put you in such a spot," she said. "I wish I felt safe enough to be here alone, but whoever put blood all over my front door knows that I'm staying here, and decided to extend the warning to me here as well."

"Don't worry about it. Tomorrow, things will be better. We'll get the supplies delivered, and we should have a good portion of the cleaning and repairs done by sundown, wouldn't you think?"

The wind blew and the rain drummed against the tin roof like a brass band.

"If you'll make us some *kaffi,* I'll build a fire to take the chill out of the air. I think the temperature dropped about ten degrees since the sun went down."

She went to the kitchen to busy her hands with making a pot of coffee, while she anticipated the warmth of a nice fire. She was a little hungry, but she feared her stomach would retaliate having even a small amount of food in it until after she calmed down. The constant loud cracks of thunder didn't help any. She jumped every time, even though she anticipated it after the lightning strike.

She'd not felt safe most of her life, but now, she felt a total state of unrest. Though she missed her parents, they'd been like strangers, almost as if not related to her. An only child of Amish parents, they were always at odds, and even more-so with the community. Her *mamm* and *daed* had even seemed mismatched, but she struggled to remember why. They were quiet—except when they'd argued, thinking she couldn't hear them.

What was it they would argue about?

If only she could remember the things she hadn't wanted to, or even intended to block out. All she really knew was that her childhood home had never felt like *home* because of the tension there. There had always been an unknown source of strife between her parents, and perhaps the deaths of her parents and the man who'd hunted them had been the reason, but what was it that nagged at her so? Was she remembering things wrong?

She stood at the sink, staring blankly out at the swaying cornstalks, a shiver running through her as the lightning illuminated the cornfield. Thunder rolled, shaking the house, and then another flicker illuminated a dark figure—a man.

She slowly turned, glancing over her shoulder, but Caleb was not at the hearth.

She opened her mouth to scream, as her eyes fixed forward, searching for the figure, but he was gone.

A low groan escaped her quivering lips as she searched the darkness.

Paralyzed with fear, she was unable to move from the window as lightning illuminated the large, dark figure, as he drew closer to the window.

Her world went silent; even the thunder was muffled from the sound of her ragged breaths, which she drew into her lungs as if running a marathon.

Making another attempt to scream, she still could not find her voice.

Her eyes bulged, as she struggled to focus in the dark room, her mind searching for a way to flee the threat of harm from her stalker.

A noise from the other room startled her, and she turned in time to see Caleb entering the *dawdi haus* with an armful of firewood.

She let out the last breath she'd been holding in with a whoosh, as she peered back out the kitchen window at the swaying cornstalks.

The figure was gone.

Her thoughts switched gears as she ran past Caleb, slammed the door, and turned the lock. Whipping around to face him, she planted herself in front of the door as though to guard it from the intruder.

He dropped the bundle of wood onto the brick hearth and rushed to her side.

"What's wrong?" he asked, searching the pale figure before him as if she was a ghost.

"There w-was a man—outside the k-kitchen w-window," she stuttered.

If not for her heaving breaths and inability to reason with him, he'd probably not believe her, but one thought nagged at him.

He'd been outside just now gathering wood from the woodpile on the other side of the barn, and had not gone near the kitchen window. If he'd been approached in any way, he'd wonder if the man was a stranger, but he'd managed to escape harm.

That left only one person: his father.

Caleb shook as he pulled Amelia into his arms and smoothed her hair. "It's nothing," he tried to assure her. "You probably saw me out there when I went to get the firewood. There isn't anyone out there, or I would have seen them. I'm certain you're over-stressed from everything that's happened today. Try to get some rest, and I'll finish building the fire."

"Don't leave," she cried. "Promise you won't leave!"

"I won't leave," he said kissing her hair. He loved her, and couldn't bear to see her so distressed, especially when he was helpless to prevent it.

He promised with a heavy heart, wondering why his own flesh and blood would go to such lengths to scare Amelia.

Chapter 10

"Are you certain this is what you want to do?" he asked as he steered Chestnut toward her farm.

Caleb couldn't help but think they were making a big mistake. She'd kept him awake most of the night with nightmares, and when she wasn't screaming in her sleep, she was pacing the floors nervously, checking all the curtains to be sure they were completely closed. He was certain his father knew he hadn't spent the night in the main house, and he knew a lecture behind the barn was on the man's mind, even though he'd been too old for his *daed's* lectures for some years.

Amelia forced herself to watch the cornfield as they rode past it, trying hard to convince herself it was only a cornfield, and the stalks would be gone soon with winter approaching.

"I need to have a place to live. Your *daed* has made it clear that I'm not welcome at your *haus,* and I'm an overtired wreck. I don't think I'll be able to sleep ever again if I don't face this."

She was shaking again, and he hated seeing her like that.

Caleb sighed heavily. He didn't want to do anything that would hurt her, and he feared this move was just too much for her to handle mentally. If he had his way, he'd protect her from all of this and take her away from it all. Point was, she owned the house, and until she either gave up on it and decided to sell the dilapidated property, or walked cleanly away, they were on a course for more nightmares and sleepless nights. The only real solution, in Caleb's opinion, was to fix the home and make it look nothing like it had when she remembered it as a child.

He clicked to Chestnut once more, urging the horse forward before he changed his mind. When they pulled into the property, a truck waited for them.

"The delivery is here," he said, trying to sound enthusiastic.

He could see by the bewildered look on her face she wasn't buying into his feigned enthusiasm, but he would keep trying to make the chore as light on the nerves as he possibly could.

A young man jumped out of the truck and greeted them. "I'm Kyle, were you expecting a delivery today?"

"*Jah*—yes," Caleb said.

He looked at Caleb, and then over at Amelia. "I need a signature from the home-owner."

"That would be me," Amelia said.

Kyle raised an eyebrow at her as he held up his clipboard. "My paperwork says Silas Graber."

Amelia's throat constricted. "That's my *daed*," she whispered. "How do you have his name on there? He's been dead eight years!"

His green eyes bore into her with a frightening familiarity that sent a shiver through her. "I'm sorry, Miss. His name was probably in our system, and when you ordered the supplies and gave this address, it probably generated an automated ticket for the delivery."

She didn't ever remember her father ordering materials from the lumber yard when she was a child, but she supposed he'd had to have ordered something at least once for them to have his name in their system. She let the matter drop, and signed for the materials with a shaky hand that did not go unnoticed by Kyle.

Surprisingly, he found her to be quite pretty—for an Amish girl. He wasn't here for pleasure; he had business to take care of, and there would be no personal mingling between him and the attractive young woman.

After checking her signature, he tossed the clipboard onto the front seat and went around back of the truck to begin unloading.

Caleb approached him. "Would you like some help?"

Kyle held up a hand. "I'd be okay with that, but the company tells me I have to unload on my own, and whatever the homeowner does with it after that is his—or *her* business," he said, as his gaze traveled over to Amelia.

Caleb didn't like the way Kyle was looking at Amelia; it sent a warning straight to the pit of his gut. "I'll leave you to your work, then."

He walked back to the buggy and urged Amelia to go inside the house with him. They stepped up to the porch with the cleaning supplies they'd brought with them, and she stood at the door, not wanting to go in.

"Are you going to be able to go in?" he asked when he saw her hesitation.

Kyle brought the panels of tin roof to the porch, pausing to look at Amelia. "Do you have a key?"

She looked up at him and nodded. "I'm having a tough time going into the house," she said, quietly. "Too many ghosts of the past."

She hadn't meant to share with the stranger; it just sort of spilled from her tongue like a bad taste she needed to spit out.

"I don't blame you. I heard the people who lived here were bank robbers!"

"My parents did not rob that bank!" Amelia shot back. "So you heard wrong!"

She'd heard the rumors about her parents, but she knew better. That man who shot them had mistaken them for someone else, and that mistake had cost her everything.

"Sorry," Kyle mumbled. "I didn't mean to get your feathers in a ruffle!"

His misuse of the expression set her nerves on edge almost as much as his ignorance about her parents' innocence. She was, in fact, so annoyed by him that she turned the lock on the door and walked inside just to spite him. His comments were not going to get the better of her. If she was to survive in the limbo state that was her life, she was going to have to get thicker skin. With one foot in the Amish community, and one foot in the *English* world, she would likely suffer ridicule from every angle, and she would have to prepare herself for what would surely come her way if she decided to reside here.

She set her things down on the living room floor and looked around. The room seemed somehow different at this moment. Perhaps it was the quietness of the place, or maybe that the floor was devoid of the blood-stained rug. Whatever it was that had suddenly changed for her, she was finally eager to get the place cleaned and painted so she could move in. She hoped a new coat of paint on the walls would brighten up the rooms, and rid the home of the musty smell.

"I suppose I'll get to work on the roof so it'll stop leaking onto the floor, but I'll have to fix this hole in the ceiling too," he said, pointing up to where water still dripped into the bucket at his feet.

"You aren't going to tackle that roof on your own, are you?" Kyle asked.

Caleb thought about it for a moment, realizing he would have to. Without the help of the community, he was on his own. His cousins still spoke to him occasionally, but they would surely be shunned too if the Bishop were to see them helping him with Amelia's roof.

"I don't have anyone else to help me besides Amelia, and I don't want her on the roof."

"I'd be more than happy to help," he offered. "This was the only delivery I had today. I do it as a favor for my uncle, who owns the lumber yard. My regular job is roofing."

"That's a kind offer, but I'm afraid we don't have money to pay you," Caleb said.

"I'm trying to establish my own business," Kyle said. "So if you'll allow me to put my sign in the yard as advertisement, I'd be willing to help you out. If you were to throw in a few meals; that would be payment enough for me."

Caleb shot Amelia a pleading look. He could tell by her expression she wasn't wild about the idea, but gave him a relenting nod just the same.

She knew Caleb could use the help, but she didn't like the way Kyle spoke to her, and the way he looked at her set her teeth on edge.

"So your uncle owns the lumber yard?" Amelia asked.

"Yeah, he's my mom's brother. He took me in when she died."

"So he raised you?" she asked curiously.

Caleb flashed her a look to mind her own business, but there was something about Kyle she didn't trust, and she was smart enough to know that if a person was trying to hide something, they wouldn't divulge personal information to a stranger.

"Only for four years, until I turned eighteen. My mother took an overdose of sleeping pills when my father died. It was too much for her."

This piqued her curiosity.

"You lost both your parents at once?" she asked.

"No, my dad left me when I was four years old—not of his own free will. He went to jail for a crime he didn't commit, and when he got out, he was killed."

Amelia felt her throat constrict. There was something too familiar about his story.

"What did you say your last name was?"

"Sinclair," he answered.

Unable to put her finger on just what it was that she didn't trust about Kyle, she pushed her inquiry a little further.

"How did your dad die?"

She knew it was rude to ask, but his story was too close to hers. She had to know.

"I didn't hear details, since he wasn't part of my life. I only know what my mom said before she died."

"And what was that?" She asked.

She knew she was pushing the issue too far, but she wasn't about to stop now. She was on to something, she knew it. She could feel it right down to the marrow in her bones. She knew the burden of proof would be on her, but she was determined to prove there was a connection, somehow. It wasn't a coincidence that he was here now, offering his help, but what was it that he sought?

"My mother told me that he was innocent of the charges against him," Kyle said.

"What was it he was charged with?" she asked, pushing him even further.

"Armed robbery," he answered.

"How can you be so sure of his innocence?" she asked.

"How can you be so sure of *your* parents' innocence?" he shot back at her.

"Because the man who really did it shot both of them right in front of me!"

"That's enough, Amelia," Caleb scolded her.

She flashed him a dirty look. "I'm just getting started," she said, her voice raised. "It seems to me that our parents have something in common, and I'm going to find out just what that is."

"I think it's only a coincidence," Kyle offered. "Why don't we drop the subject and get to work on the house. We won't get to the entire roof today, especially since it's supposed to rain later this afternoon. I think we should work on getting as much of that roof covered as possible before the rain comes."

Amelia leered at him. He was indeed hiding something. Was it possible he was the son of the man she shot? Was it possible he was behind all the mischief? Somehow, facing her terrorizer made it a little easier for her to accept. If he was up to something, she would be ready for him.

"I agree," Caleb said. "Let's get that roof done."

Kyle excused himself to get the last load of materials from his truck.

"What was that all about?" Caleb asked her once Kyle was out of earshot.

"Whose side are you on?" she accused.

"I'm on your side, always," he said. "But don't you think you were unnecessarily rude to him? I need his help, and now I'll be lucky if he stays and helps me with the roof."

"You don't think this story matches mine almost exactly?" She asked him.

"No, I don't! I think you're losing control of your emotions," he said. "You're becoming paranoid."

"Who wouldn't be under these circumstances? But I'm not paranoid," she shot back. "You heard him. He's hiding something."

"You can't be sure of that," Caleb defended Kyle. "Besides, even if he is related to the man who killed your parents, that doesn't make him a murderer too. And how do you explain the fact he doesn't even have the same last name as the man who killed your parents?"

"He could have easily lied. It makes me suspicious of him. You don't think it's awfully fishy that he's here? Or the fact that he knew my father owned this house?"

"I'll admit that is a strange coincidence, but don't you worry; I'll be keeping my eye on him. In the meantime, keep your mouth shut. You don't want to make him think you suspect him."

"I will do no such thing, Caleb Yoder, and you can't make me. I think he's behind the blood on my door and the blood in your *dawdi haus*. I suspect him of everything, and I want you to make him leave."

Caleb reflected on his suspicions of his father. "Somehow," he said. "I don't think Kyle is responsible for that."

"How do you figure?" she asked.

Caleb looked at his feet, feeling shame rising up in his cheeks, heating them. "Because I just don't. When you went back to the bedroom when I removed the rug. My dad came to the door, and he had on his leather apron and rubber boots. He'd just slaughtered two pigs."

Amelia's breath hitched, and tears pooled in her eyes. "That doesn't *prove* anything, does it?"

"Not by itself, except it came with a warning. He warned me again to get you off of the property," Caleb continued quietly. "I have to wonder if he did it just to scare you. I'm sorry, and I'm ashamed to think my *daed* could have done such a thing, but I don't think Kyle is the one you need to worry about. I think we need to get your place finished so we can get you settled in here before my father goes off the deep end."

Amelia studied Caleb's dark blue eyes. The sparkle had gone from them, and his ashen face held a sorrow she could not bear. She closed the space between them and he wrapped his arms around her, kissing her hair. He would protect her, even if it meant defending her against his own father.

Chapter 11

Amelia took a step back to look at her clean kitchen.
She'd spent the entire day disinfecting everything
from floor to ceiling, and she was proud of her
progress. She was now ready to paint since the
living room would have to wait until after they
finished the roof. The leaks in there had caused
damage that would involve repairing the ceiling and
possibly the floorboards in some areas. Though she
knew it would be close to a week before she would
be able to move in, she knew each day would bring
her closer to the freedom she'd wanted for the past
eight years.

"Where do you want me to put the paint, Amish girl?" Kyle asked, startling her from her reverie.

Amelia felt her heart pounding all the way down to her toes. She sucked in a breath, heaving it in as if she couldn't get any air.

"You alright, little Amish girl?" Kyle asked.

"Why—are you calling me that?" she pleaded, through ragged breaths.

It was the way he'd said it that reminded her of that night when Bruce was chasing her through the cornfield.

He held up his hands defensively. "I didn't mean any disrespect," he said. "I just forgot your name, that's all. Don't shoot me or anything!"

"Why would you think I'd shoot you?" she asked through gritted teeth.

"I didn't mean anything by it," he said. "Like I said little Amish girl, I just forgot your name, that's all."

"Don't ever call me little Amish girl again!"

He chuckled. "Sorry!"

"I don't find any of this funny. Maybe you should leave. I'm sure Caleb can finish the roof on his own. We don't need your help."

Just then Caleb burst through the door holding up a bloodied hand.

Amelia screamed. "What happened?" she asked, rushing to his side.

"I was trying to move the panels of roof from the pallet to put them on the porch," he said hastily. "The wind caught them and they tore into my hands. There's an awful storm headed our way, and I was trying to put everything away. It startled me so much that I dropped the pallet, and I think I broke two of my fingers."

Kyle rushed to his side with a clean shop-cloth he picked up from the top of the stack, and wrapped it around Caleb's hand. "Let me take a look," he said, as he mopped up some of the blood. "Wiggle your fingers."

Caleb tried, but he couldn't move the last two.

"I think you're right about breaking the last two fingers," Kyle said. "But I don't think the cuts are deep enough to need stitches. When's the last time you had a tetanus shot?"

"I had to get one last year when I sliced open my leg on the plow, so I'm covered."

"That'll save us a trip to the emergency room," Kyle said. "Unfortunately, you're not gonna be able to do that roof now, I'll have to finish it myself."

Amelia narrowed her eyes at him. She had just ordered him to leave her home, and now it seemed she would need him to stay. The thought of it aggravated her.

Caleb winced as he applied pressure to the cuts.

"Let's go outside to my truck," Kyle said. "I think I have a first-aid kit out there."

When they went out the front door, Amelia could see the black sky from the doorway, and the wind had picked up. Caleb was right about the impending storm. She was ready to quit for the day anyway, but she wasn't looking forward to riding back with Kyle. They'd left the horse and buggy for Caleb's *daed* so he could go into town when they'd gone back for lunch, leaving them stranded in the storm if they didn't ride back with Kyle.

A sudden darkness fell over the house, adding a deep chill to the air. Lightning flashed, and thunder rolled in the distance, and it made her shiver. Rain began to pelt down onto the tin roof, and within minutes, it was dripping onto the living room floor again. She dashed across the wood floor toward the galvanized bucket to put it under the spot that was dripping the heaviest, her foot falling through the boards with a snap.

She cried out in pain, as she collapsed onto the wet floor. Pulling her twisted ankle loose from the floorboard, the plank of wood popped up. Although she was crying from the pain, she noticed something between the floorboards, and leaned in for a closer look. There was no mistaking the large canvas bag wedged in the dirty cocoon, water stains marring it from the leaky roof and years of lying in wait of being discovered.

Panic seized her as she leaned over the decayed floorboard to move the bag. She knew it was filled with money from the worn lettering on the front. It boasted the name of the bank downtown; the one that was robbed more than eighteen years ago.

What was it doing under the floorboards of her house?

"Are you okay?" Kyle asked from the doorway.

Amelia instinctively grabbed the piece of flooring and replaced it before he came any closer. "My foot found a loose board and I think I sprained my ankle," she answered, trying to act casual.

He crouched down on his haunches next to her and picked up her foot, touching the ankle gently. "I think you're right. It's beginning to swell, but it's probably only a sprain. The bone doesn't seem to be broken."

She pulled her foot away, feeling uncomfortable at his lingering touch.

He remained on his haunches and peered at the loose board that now covered the hidden money. She backed away nervously, wondering if she could get up and leave.

Remaining where he was, Kyle looked at her curiously, and cocked his head to one side. "I sprained my ankle once when I was younger," he began. "It was when I was four years old. My dad had taken me fishing—he used to take me fishing all the time, but this time I accidentally stepped in the bucket of bait when I backed into it trying to reel in a big fish. I tipped it over and my ankle twisted. I'll never forget that day; it was the last day I saw my dad alive."

His story made Amelia nervous, and she backed away even further, checking behind her to remember where the door was, should she need to escape.

"When my father went to prison," he continued. "My mother became addicted to pills of all kinds. Pain pills, sleeping pills, you name it. Things might've been easier for us if we'd had the money my father was accused of stealing. As it was, he claimed all along that it was four Amish kids that took the money. They never did catch those kids."

Amelia knew better than to interrupt him, and so she remained quiet, all the while, trying to think of how she would escape with her sprained ankle.

"My dad went to prison for ten long years, while those Amish kids spent that money."

"Where's Caleb?" she interrupted nervously.

He chuckled. "I sent him home to get bandages. There weren't any in my truck after all!"

Amelia's spine went cold, and her brain numb, as if someone had filled her veins with ice water. She could feel her heart racing, and she tried to scoot away from him with her left foot, her right foot unable to maneuver because of the pain. His story had gone from making her nervous, to terrifying her, for she feared that Kyle was Bruce's son. Was he telling her his sad story so he could justify it when he killed her?

She wanted to tell him where the money was, but it was not hers to give to him. He was wrong about her parents spending the money; it was still down between the floorboards only a few inches from where he stood.

There was only one thing that still nagged at her; if her parents were two of the Amish kids that took the money, who were the other two?

****

Caleb tiptoed through the house, not wanting to alert his dad to his presence there. He was in a hurry, not wanting to leave Amelia alone with Kyle for too long. He didn't have any reason not to trust him, but Amelia was leery of him, and if she found out he was gone, she would surely be upset with him. As he wandered through the house to the upstairs bathroom where he knew there were bandages, he could faintly hear his father mumbling from down the hall. He stepped closer to his father's room, listening to the man's ramblings.

"We should never have spent that money we stole," his father mumbled. "We should have turned it in before anyone was hurt."

Was there someone in there with him?

"That money has cursed us, Lord, and I regret not turning it in when I had the chance."

Had he heard his father correctly? It seemed that his father was praying—no—confessing to a robbery. How was that possible? He strained to listen some more.

"My gun took a man's life, Lord, and the guilt has never left me. I put that gun in my own hands and held it against innocent people and stole money that didn't belong to me. Please forgive me and lift this burden from me."

Caleb felt his heart pounding against his ribcage. His father had told the authorities he had no idea where the gun had come from. He'd lied to them— and to his own son about that night. Rumors had circulated around the community about the involvement of four Amish kids that had committed the crime during their *rumspringa,* and how they'd helped an *Englisher* rob a bank. He never thought his own parents could be involved.

Was it really possible his parents were part of that foursome?

"We were just kids," his father continued to ramble on. "But I've lived with the guilt all these years. Forgive me, Lord. Forgive me for having a gun that took a man's life, and forgive me for helping to steal that money. Forgive me for spending it."

Caleb felt fear rise up like bile from his stomach. He could taste the stickiness of adrenaline on his tongue. He had to get out of the house. Had to get away from the reality that was hitting him full-force. How was he going to break the news to Amelia that his own father was involved in the same robbery from which her parents had lost their lives? How would he tell her that it was his father that had splattered the blood all over to scare her away? Had it all been to save him from the shame of the past? He prayed for the words to say to her as he hitched up Chestnut to his father's buggy.

****

Amelia rose from the floor. "I think I can walk on my ankle if I don't put too much pressure on it," she said nervously, trying to change the subject away from Kyle's rendition of the robbery and shootings.

His offended expression let her know he wouldn't be distracted from finishing what he had to say. "We would have had the money and a good life if *you* hadn't shot my father!"

Amelia could feel the blood draining from her limbs. She blinked rapidly against the flashes of lightning that illuminated Kyle, his silhouette mirroring his father's on the night she'd shot him.

"I'm sorry. I didn't mean to kill him," she pleaded with trembling lips. "I was only a little girl. I didn't mean to shoot him. The gun went off by accident."

She took a step back, stumbling against the pain in her ankle.

Kyle reached out to her, but she flinched away.

"I won't hurt you, little Amish girl," he said, holding a hand out to her.

She turned on her heels, pain stabbing her ankle, but she pushed it down; her fight-or-flight response choosing to flee.

Taking the same labored steps she'd traveled on that terrible night eight years ago, she limped and hobbled, her only goal to put distance between herself and Kyle. She mentally traveled the same trail through the cornfield to Caleb's house where she would be safe, but fear blocked the memory. Hobbling through the unfamiliar rows, her gate reminded her of her stalker's that night. He'd hobbled, and it had cost him valuable time in catching her.

This time, she was the one losing valuable time.

Whimpering uncontrollably with ragged breaths, she maneuvered through the narrow rows, struggling to remember the path that would lead to safety. She could hear her *mamm's* voice floating over the tops of the tassels, calling to her, but her mother's ghost was guiding her back toward danger.

Ignoring her *mamm's* voice and the voices of the past that haunted her, she continued to stumble through the dips and rises in the soil, while the autumn-dried stalks whipped the flesh of her cheeks and arms. She ignored the stinging pain; her goal to reach the edge of the cornfield that connected her property with Caleb's farm. She still had a ways to go after she exited the cornfield before she would reach his farmhouse, but she continued to run, her instincts the only thing guiding her through the maze that encompassed her.

Sudden pain assaulted her, stinging her flesh as she became entangled in the barbed-wire fence that separated her from Caleb and his property. Lightning flashed, and she scanned the cornrows behind her for signs of the one who hunted her like a wild animal.

Desperately tugging at the wires that held her arms, the spikes ripped open her flesh and sunk deeper, holding her hostage.

She choked down the screams she knew would be a beacon to her location, as she made another painful attempt at freeing herself from the shackles that imprisoned her.

It was all in vain…she was trapped!

Chapter 12

Kyle didn't waste any time unearthing what had been resting beneath the floorboards. He could tell by Amelia's nervous reaction she'd found something very deep beneath them. After he pulled up several planks, he couldn't believe his eyes. There was the money all along. If only he'd found it any of the times he'd ransacked the home over the years while it had laid vacant.

He chuckled and talked aloud to the bag as if it understood him. "I suppose I should be glad I didn't find you before, or I would still be tempted to keep you."

He paused. "This money isn't any more mine than it is Amelia's, or anyone else's. It needs to go back to where it was stolen from; the bank."

He pulled the dampened bag from betwixt the floorboards and let it drop to the floor with a thud.

"I don't know how my father managed to get ahold of all this money, but I hope that wherever he is now, he's realized it wasn't worth losing his life over. I hope he knows it wasn't worth the lives of two other innocent people."

"Correction!" A female voice said from behind him. "That would be *three* innocent lives."

Kyle whipped his head around to the female figure standing in the dark doorway, lightning illuminating her angry silhouette.

"I take it you're Bruce's kid?" she asked him casually.

Kyle nodded.

"I hate to break it to you, but your father was just as guilty as we were. We all stole that money equally, and we were supposed to divide it equally, but your father stole something from me that was far more precious to me than that money," she said bitterly. "Something I can never get back; my husband and my daughter!"

"Are you Amelia's mom?" Kyle asked as he stood, the bag of money at his feet.

She walked in through the door, a pistol trained on him, while scanning between him and the bag of money.

"I'm the woman that your father made a childless widow over this money, and I should think that I'm entitled to that money to make up for my losses. He killed my only child."

"Are you Amelia's mother?" He asked again, taking note of her modern attire. Wearing a pair of jeans and a T-shirt, her clothing was nothing like the conservative *Amish* garb her daughter and Caleb had worn. Her gray and brown-streaked hair was down and rested on her shoulders, unlike Amelia's, which she wore tightly bound at the nape of her neck, and covered by a white *kapp*.

"I *was* her mother," she said bitterly.

But she's not dea…, he tried to say, but she cocked the gun, causing him to raise his hands defensively.

He didn't dare say another word, although he felt it necessary to tell her that her daughter was still alive. Didn't she know?

Before Kyle could think about giving her the good news, she tossed a thick rope at him, and ordered him to sit in her old rocking chair—the only chair in the room.

"Tie your feet to the chair, and make sure the rope is real tight," she said, pointing the gun at him.

"Don't do this," he begged, as he obeyed her demand. "Take the money, but please let me go!"

"I already intend to take the money! It's mine! I'll have to give you kudos for finding *my* money. I've wondered where it was for more than eighteen long years, but I never thought my husband would hide the money under the floorboards. He kept that money from me all those years, making us scrimp and save to pay back every penny of it. I worked my fingers to the bone sewing quilts until my fingers bled, and crocheting blankets and mittens and hats and scarves, and everything in-between, while he made harnesses and furniture for local shops. We slaved all those years to pay back all that money— the money we spent on our humble little farm. Now look at it." She turned her nose up as she looked around her home with disgust. "Before my husband had a chance to turn it in, your father found us and, well, you know the rest—no sense in repeating it!"

When she was satisfied his legs were securely tied to the chair legs, she ordered him to put his arms behind him. Then she wrapped the loop of a slip-knot around his wrists and pulled it tight.

Kyle winced against the pain, the ropes cutting off his circulation. The older woman was certainly strong, he'd have to give her that.

"That's tight enough so you can't get loose," she said, laughing.

"Don't do this," he begged again.

Ignoring his pleas, she grabbed the bottles of kerosene for the lanterns and began to splash it against the walls, and all the while, Kyle was pleading for his life.

"I'll be happy to see this place go up in flames," she said, continuing to ignore his non-stop begging and alternate whimpering. "For a lot of years, I've wanted to rid myself of the prison this house became for me and my family as we slaved to pay back the money. All it did was make me angry. After I woke up in the hospital, they told me Amelia and my husband had both been killed, and after the funerals, they put me in witness protection. I've been stuck there all this time, and they suddenly let me out for some strange reason."

"You don't have to be angry," Kyle said. "Amelia is alive! She just left here. She went through the cornfield out back. She went to Caleb's house!"

"You're a liar, just like your father! She's dead and buried. I saw the casket myself."

"Let me go and I'll prove it to you! She's alive. I just spoke to her!"

"Liar, liar, pants on fire!" she sang.

Then, picking up the money, she stood at the doorway and flashed Kyle a pleased look, and then struck a match.

"NO! Wait!" he half-cried. "Please! Why are you doing this?"

"An eye for an eye!" she said, flicking the match behind her.

Chapter 13

Caleb coughed and choked, his eyes tearing up from the autumn air that filled his nostrils with the stench of smoke. Burning leaves was something he disliked the most about the season, but this smell was somehow different. It didn't smell like burning leaves; it smelled much stronger. The smoke filled his lungs, and would surely make his asthma worse.

He climbed inside the buggy and clicked to Chestnut, steering him down the road toward Amelia's house.

As he headed down the long lane toward the main road, he could see smoke rising over the top of the thick tree-line. It seemed to be coming from the direction of Amelia's house.

"Oh, *Gott,* please--*nooooo*!"

Caleb's cry rent the air, splitting the dead of night, but it wasn't enough to stop the inevitable. There was no one to call for help, no one to hear his pleas that echoed against the acres of farmland that separated him from the nearest farmhouse.

Panic filled him at the thought of something happening to Amelia, and he slapped the reins against his horse's hind flank, urging him into a fast trot. If Amelia was in danger, he'd never be able to forgive himself for leaving her alone with Kyle. She'd begged him to let him go from his employ, but he hadn't listened. She'd warned him that there was something fishy going on, and he'd put her concerns off, thinking only of himself and the help he needed with the roof.

He prayed haphazardly as he urged the horse to go faster still, being careless and unaware of the possibility of cars being on the dark, country road with him. Lightning flashed, illuminating the dark silhouette of her house, and what was left of the roof. Flames licked the blackened sky, Caleb fearing he'd never make it in time to save her. His breath came out in short spurts as he prayed for her safety.

****

Kyle teetered and rocked the chair back-and-forth until he tipped it over, crashing down hard against his shoulder. The impact dislocated his shoulder, sending a surge of pain through his entire body. But he knew if he didn't risk the injury, he would soon not be able to breathe. His only hope of possible survival was to get low to the floor below the smoke-line.

Mere seconds after the fall, he rolled onto his back, and then over to his good shoulder; the one he hadn't fallen on. He began to scissor kick his torso to scoot closer to the door. He had no idea how he would get out of the house when he got there, but perhaps he would have to break one of the low windows with his feet.

Knowing it was better to get a few cuts and scrapes than to lose his life, he worked quickly to get free from the burning house. He coughed and choked and sputtered, heaving in smoky breaths that burned his lungs. He knew he needed to work quickly, or the chances of him getting out of the house alive were slimmer with each second that passed.

He could already hear the creak from the floor that would give way under him. The walls and the ceiling were in flames, and he could hear the creaking of the roof collapsing.

****

Caleb pushed his gelding as far as the animal would go, his ears twitching, and his steps sporadic as he tried to avoid going any further. Chestnut whinnied and nickered, his hooves pawing at the pavement. The animal's instincts warned his owner of the danger of getting too close to the flaming house.

Caleb turned the buggy around and jumped out, knowing the horse would go back home.

"Go on, boy," he said, as he slapped the horse on the flank. "Go home."

Caleb ran the rest of the way, his lungs filling with smoke, his heart-rate so rapid he felt nauseated.

When the house came into view, he was shocked to see the roof engulfed in flames. He feared the worst, concerned that Amelia might already be dead inside the home, consumed with smoke inhalation.

Still, he ran fast to reach the house, hearing a faint call for help, but it wasn't a feminine voice. It was Kyle's voice and not Amelia's. Confusion plagued him over the desperate, and ragged call for help from Kyle.

Working his way through the tall grass up to the porch, he could see there would be no saving the house, but he prayed he could save Amelia and Kyle.

Even at the edge of the property, he could feel the heat from the fire like the burn of the afternoon sun on his face. The smoke was so thick it burned his lungs, forcing him into a fit of coughing.

He approached the burning building with caution, putting an arm up to shield his eyes from the almost blinding arc of fire. The crackling of the flames, and the roaring heat were overbearing. His heart heavy, he already mourned for Amelia, his fears unable to rest until he knew where she was.

He yelled out hoping he would hear the faint cries that he'd heard as he approached.

"I'm here," Kyle called him. "By the door."

Caleb stepped up onto the front porch, completely aware that the house could collapse at any moment. He put his hand up on the door feeling the warmth, but it wasn't too hot to the touch. The front window had been cracked and black smoke billowed out, blinding his view of the inside of the home.

He pushed open the door slowly and there was Kyle, wriggling on the floor, tied to a chair. He was coughing and choking, and his eyes were swollen and weeping.

He looked up at Caleb with relief in his tear-filled eyes. "Help me! Hurry! Get me out of here!

"Where's Amelia?" Caleb hollered over the roar of the fire.

"She ran over to your place almost half an hour ago. You didn't see her?" Kyle said, choking.

"No!"

Caleb grabbed a hold of the rocking chair and dragged him out of the house as fast as he could, unconcerned when he bumped him down each step of the porch. He dragged him fast into the yard, aware that Kyle was howling from the pain.

"I'm sorry Kyle," he said, loosening the ropes that bound him to the chair. "Where's Amelia? Are you sure she's not in the house?"

"Yes, I'm sure. She ran across the field almost half an hour ago."

"Did she do this to you? Did she tie you to this chair?" he asked.

"No! It was Amelia's mother!" he said, coughing.

"What do you mean, Amelia's mother? She's dead!"

"No she isn't! She was trying to barbeque me!"

"Why did she set the house on fire?"

Kyle coughed really hard, pushing the last of the smoke from his lungs. "She said it was to get back at my dad for killing her husband and daughter. She thinks Amelia is dead!"

"So you really are Bruce Albee's son?"

Kyle nodded. "I used my mother's maiden name—
the same name as my uncle because Albee isn't
such a respected name in these parts."

"Did Amelia take off running when she saw her
mother?"

Kyle hung his head in shame. "No! I'm afraid I
might have scared her, but I was just a little freaked
out. I would never harm her, but I don't think she
knows that."

"What happened?"

"Amelia's mother took the money!"

"What money?" Caleb asked, feeling a little
confused.

"Amelia found the money from the robbery in the
floorboards. I freaked out when I saw the bag of
money, and it made me mad seeing it, just thinking
of everything we've all lost. I believed in my dad's
innocence all my life, but now I know it wasn't true.
He was guilty, and we need to get the money from
Amelia's mom and turn it in."

Caleb stood back and looked at his beloved
Amelia's home. Smoke billowed up against the full

moon, the flames illuminating the air against the expanse of farmland where it seemed to pause just before melting into the horizon. Bending, creaking, and the crashing sound of breaking glass filled his ears. He was certain there would be no love-loss between the property and Amelia.

"I don't know how she's going to feel about this," he said, unable to turn away from the burning house.

Kyle coughed and wiped soot from his cheeks. "I think we should try to find her before her mother catches up to her. There's no telling what the woman will do."

"I'm worried about her. She could be in danger. The woman could hurt her."

Kyle twisted at the rope burns on his wrists, coughing one last, good cough. "Or try to barbeque her!"

"Are you able to go with me, or should I go by myself?"

"I can go. Do you want me to call the fire department?"

Caleb nodded, wiping the sweat from his brow. He had no idea how much heat a burning house generated.

"Call the police too. Her mom tried to burn you alive, and she took the money. Those are two very serious things."

Kyle dialed 911 from his cell phone, thankful that Amelia's mom hadn't thought to take it from him.

Chapter 14

Amelia tried in vain to break free from the entanglement of the barbed-wire, her arms and legs immovable against the deep cuts that held her tightly bound against the fence. Her energy spent, she could no longer move, nor could she escape.

She was defeated against the strength of her barbed-wire captor.

She would wait for Kyle to come and do his worst, and then perhaps finally, the ghosts of the past would be put to rest. Unable to run from her assailant, she waited, her heart barely beating.

She could hear the faint call of her *mamm* floating over the tops of the tassels in the cornfield. The voice whispered gently, calling her home.

Gusts of wind brought waves of memories rustling over the rows of dried cornstalks. She didn't want to think about the past at this moment, but a picture of her parents entered her mind—a happy time, when life felt safe, and the sun shined every day. It was a silly memory that fogged her thinking, but in her mind she needed safety, so she could face what would happen next.

She knew she didn't have much time, and all she could do was whisper a faint prayer, hoping that the current of air would carry her message along the fast-moving storm clouds, and up to heaven where it would be heard.

Blood drained from her wounds, and she shivered against the numbness and cold she now felt. It wouldn't be long, and all her ghosts would be put to rest.

"I'm here *mamm,*" she whispered faintly, answering the call from her mother. "I'm here, and I'm waiting for you to take me home."

Coming upon the clearing in the tall cornstalks, Abigail Graber gasped at the slip of a figure the lightning illuminated before her. The young woman resembled her daughter, and she cried out to her, lifting her only free arm, but then it dropped weakly to the ground.

"Melia?"

Her mother set down the bag of money and knelt down beside her daughter, gently unraveling the hem of her dress, giving her room to move more freely.

Unwrapping a slack wire from around her arm, she left the tines stuck in her wrist, knowing that to remove it would cause Amelia to bleed to death. So instead, she pulled gently away from the post to cause more slack, the tines cutting into her own hand.

"Come here, my little Melia," she cooed her daughter, as she pulled her into her arms. "I'm here."

Amelia spotted an unfamiliar figure illuminating in the flashes of lightning, and thunder cracked, causing her to jump slightly, her senses barely aware of what was happening to her, but she somehow felt safe.

Working quickly to free her daughter from the entanglement of the wire web, she knew she was losing precious time, for Amelia had already lost a lot of blood. She would die if she wasn't careful, and if she didn't get help soon. In the distance, Abigail could hear sirens, and she knew they would be coming to put out the fire she'd started.

Abigail looked into her daughter's nearly lifeless, pale face. What had she done? They had told her that her only child was dead, but here she was in front of her, and she was holding little Amelia in her arms. She wept, not for herself, but for her child, and the fear she must've felt growing up without her mother.

"Mamm, where are you?" Amelia called out weakly.

"I'm here. Hush my Melia. Help is on the way."

Holding Amelia in her arms, Abigail glanced down at the bag of money next to her leg. Tilting her head back, she lifted her chin toward the heavens and sobbed.

"Forgive me, Lord. Deliver me from the evil this money has added to my life. Please don't let my daughter suffer for my sins. I've lost my faith, dear Lord, and I pray you'll forgive me and help me to have faith again."

She gently rocked her barely conscious daughter in her arms, seeing her only child's life slipping away.

"What have I done, Lord?" she cried out. "My greed and anger, and my need for revenge has cost me my only child. Please change my heart, and spare my child from paying for my sins," she begged.

Amelia's lashes fluttered once more, and she looked up into her *mamm's* face and whispered, "I forgive you."

Then she went limp in her mother's arms.

Chapter 15

Abigail's screams rent the air. Caleb and Kyle, who had been following the trail through the cornfield, looked at each other at the sound of the woman's screams. They knew Amelia wasn't far off, but they also knew that the scream did not come from Amelia. Caleb's mind was whirling, and he wondered if Amelia had gotten into a scuttle with her mother.

"Do you think you can run?" he asked Kyle. "I think we should hurry."

Kyle nodded and the two took off running in the direction they'd heard the screams.

When they came upon the clearing in the cornfield, Kyle was suddenly faced with the woman who'd tried to kill him. He yanked Caleb's sleeve, and pulled him back into the shadows of the cornfield. "Watch it," he warned. "She has a gun!"

They both stepped cautiously out of the cornfield, the lightning illuminating the path. When Caleb saw how bloody Amelia was, and that she lay limp in her mother's arms, he could feel his throat constricting. He loved her more than anything. He'd loved her his entire life. And now, was she... *dead*?

They both stood there in shock, unable to speak for what seemed like a small eternity.

"What did you do to her?" Kyle accused.

"I found her like this," Abigail defended herself. "Help her! I think she's dying!"

Caleb collapsed onto his haunches in front of Abigail, pulling Amelia into his arms and sobbing. Her breath hitched ever so slightly, but that was enough to put a hopeful smile on his face.

"She's alive!" he said, rushing to his feet and pulling her closely.

"Wait!" Abigail shouted. "You can't move her. The barbed-wire is the only thing keeping her from bleeding to death. It has to be cut away from the post before we can move her!"

Kyle shoved his hand deep into his jeans pocket and pulled out a screwdriver and a small pair of wire cutters.

"I don't know if these'll work," he said. "But I'm gonna try."

He worked the barbed-wire, bending it back and forth with the wire-cutters until he finally snapped the section loose. Then he wound it up and tucked it into the hem of Amelia's skirts as Caleb carried her back through the cornfield and out to the road. Police and fire trucks had assembled there with an entire rescue crew at Amelia's house to put out the fire.

Kyle began to walk behind him, but Abigail stopped him with a gentle hand on his arm.

"Please," she said. "I want to tell you that I'm sorry for what I did to you, and I'm glad you're okay. If you hadn't been here with the tools to cut my daughter free, she might have died here. Now, she has a chance. Thank you for saving her after what I did to you."

"I didn't do it for you. I did it for Amelia."

"I really am sorry for what I did."

"Tell it to the authorities, lady!" he said. "Give me the gun."

She reached into her pocket and handed it to him. "I wasn't going to shoot you."

Kyle picked up the bag of money and stepped back.

"Do I have to point the gun at you now, or are you gonna go peacefully with me?"

"It isn't loaded!" she said.

"You managed to tie me up and leave me for dead in a burning building, and the gun wasn't even loaded?"

"I told you I was sorry," she said. "I'm ready to face whatever consequences I'm due. I don't know what I was thinking. I've been so stricken with grief for the past eight years that I didn't know what I was doing. I think I need to go back to the state hospital so I can continue to get treatment because I'm not a well woman."

Kyle looked at her skeptically.

"I wasn't really in Witness Protection. I've been in the state mental institution all these years, but as long as I know that my daughter is okay, I think I'll be okay now. Being able to see her a second time has really changed me. I've locked away all the past and it's not been easy, but now that I know my daughter is alive and she's going to live I just know everything else is going to be okay too. I know because I prayed for it and I have faith now."

Chapter 16

Amelia woke up hearing faint noises that sounded the same as when she'd had her appendix out. She'd stayed a couple days in the hospital, and this sounded the same.

She breathed in deeply, smelling fresh oxygen, the feel of the cannula tucked in her nostrils. If she wasn't in the hospital, perhaps she was dead? Did being dead smell and sound the same as being in the hospital?

She let her eyes drift open, her gaze traveling around the hospital room. Caleb slept in the chair next to her bed, and she was happy to see him, but then her gaze fell on the chair seated at the foot of her bed, and she began to scream.

Caleb jumped up, startled awake. "What's wrong?"

She tried to sit up in bed, but her bandaged arms wouldn't allow her too much movement without pain.

"What's he doing here?" she asked, narrowing her eyes at Kyle.

"Everything is going to be fine, Amelia," Caleb assured her. "Kyle isn't going to hurt you. I give you my word on that."

"But he… chased me through the cornfield and… I don't remember what happened after that, but if I'm in the hospital, I want to know what he did to me?"

"He didn't chase you; he admitted to getting impatient with you and trying to scare you a little, but you ran from the house, and he didn't follow you," Caleb assured her again, patting her hand gently.

In the meantime, Kyle excused himself from the room, rubbing the sleep from his eyes. "I'm going for a cup of coffee, Caleb. Do you want one?"

Caleb nodded. *"Danki."*

Then he turned back to Amelia and tried to calm her.

"My father put up barbed-wire fence between our properties so that you couldn't get through," Caleb said. "You ran into it and cut yourself up pretty bad. You've lost a lot of blood."

"Speaking of blood. What about the blood all over my porch and on your rug in the *dawdi haus*?"

Caleb lowered his head shamefully. "My dad did that to scare you away, and he's very sorry for it. He did it to cover up his involvement in the robbery. Turns out, my parents and your parents committed the crime when they were not too much younger than we are. They were on their *rumspringa,* but that's no excuse. My father figured that if he got you to believe that someone wanted you out of the community, you would actually leave, and he could continue to hide his part in the robbery. But he came clean and turned himself in. He's at home now waiting for the decision, but his lawyer said that he thinks he's going to get him just probation."

A quiet knock sounded at the door, and Amelia looked at the woman in the doorway, her breath catching in her throat.

"*Mamm,*" she whispered, a lump clogging her throat. "Is it really you?"

The woman at the door nodded.

Was she really seeing what she thought she saw? Was it possible her *mamm* was truly alive? She thought that she'd only dreamed of her, but now it seemed she was standing in the doorway.

"Is it alright if I come see you, my little Melia?"

Amelia began to sob, and she nodded her head. She'd longed to hear her mother call her by her pet name for so many years.

Abigail sat on the edge of her bed, and Caleb excused himself from the room.

Amelia looked up into her mother's aged face, searching for the familiarity that she'd missed so much. "What happened to you? I saw Bruce shoot you! I thought you were dead."

"I almost was," she said softly. "When I woke up in the hospital, I was told you were dead. I went to your funeral."

"I was there too, but they wouldn't let me get out of the car!" Amelia said. "They told me I had to watch from the car, and when it was over, they took me to the orphanage, and that's where I stayed until about a week ago."

Abigail placed her hand over her daughter's bandaged hands and held them.

"I was so distraught with grief after having to watch my family's funeral from a state car too, that I've spent all this time in a mental institution."

Amelia cried even harder. "Oh *Mamm,* I'm so sorry you had to stay there. I wish I'd known that you were alive."

"I wish I'd known too; it might have saved us both a lot of heartache over the past eight years."

"We have the rest of our lives to make up for lost time," Amelia said, wiping her tears.

Abigail's gaze lowered. "I'm afraid we don't," she said, holding up her right arm showing off a thick, locked bracelet on her arm. "At least not yet. And that's if you still want anything to do with me after you hear what I have to say."

"You sound so serious," Amelia said.

Abigail tucked her daughter's wispy brown hair behind her ear, trying to savor the moment before she risked it all with the truth. "I'd rather you heard this from me, so, here goes! I'm afraid I'm on lockdown for a little while. Like I said, I've been in a state facility for mentally ill patients, and I need to continue to stay there for a while. The only reason I'm here now, is because they're holding me over in the psychiatric ward here at the hospital while you're here. They think it'll be good for my therapy, and I agree with them. I've never felt better."

"Now that you know that I'm alive you should be okay, shouldn't you?"

Abigail couldn't even look her daughter in the eye.

"I'm afraid not," she said quietly. "I burned down the house—our house—*your* house."

"I don't care!" Amelia said. "That place is tainted with ghosts of the past. We need to start fresh. What's the problem?"

"The problem is," Abigail said shamefully. "Is that I tied Kyle up in the house and left him there after lighting a match, and setting the house ablaze. I left him there to die!" she said, sobbing.

Amelia sucked in a breath. "Why would you do such a thing, *Mamm?*" she asked quietly.

"It's not one of my prouder moments, but neither is robbing a bank when I was seventeen. I wanted to hurt Kyle because I hurt so much that I wanted revenge, and I felt his father was responsible. I wanted to avenge your death and your father's death. I wasn't thinking straight, and I know this now."

She held up the bracelet and smiled, grief still clouding her thoughts. "I'm going to get the right help, and now that I know you're okay, I'll be okay."

Amelia hugged her mother, savoring the moment, and making plans in her head to keep in close contact with the woman. She loved her *mamm,* despite her many faults, and there was nothing that would ever change that.

Chapter 17

"They're here!" Amelia said excitedly, as she positioned and repositioned the flowers on the table. She wanted everything to be perfect. She'd set out tea, using her best teacups, and she couldn't wait for her *mamm* to see the new house that her betrothed, Caleb, and his business partner, Kyle, had built for their future. Running a hand along her *mamm's* rocking chair—the only item that had survived the fire, she couldn't wait for her to see how nicely Caleb had restored it. She'd told *mamm* about salvaging the chair from the yard amidst the rubble before the mess from the fire was cleared, and her *mamm* had told her she could have the chair to rock her future grandchildren in, and that she wanted the chair to create a happy memory for her. Amelia had to admit that it looked nice positioned next to the brick hearth that Caleb had tried his best to duplicate from her childhood home—only this one was devoid of ghosts from the past. She smiled, unwilling to let anything spoil this day for her.

Straightening pleats of her newly sewn, blue dress, and tucking a stray tendril up underneath her prayer *kapp*, she pulled in a deep breath, determined not to let her nervousness show. Caleb's dad had been released from his ninety-day sentence a few days earlier, but he would be on probation for three years. He'd taken the buggy to go pick up her *mamm* from the bus station. Although yesterday was her release day, she decided to wait until today, her daughter's wedding day, to make her first visit. Amelia and Caleb, and even Kyle, had been to visit her several times at the facility, and had even sat with her during a few of her therapy sessions. It had helped Amelia a great deal with the nightmares that had plagued her.

Thanks to the sessions, and her new life, she hadn't had a nightmare in close to two months. They had slowly dwindled away after she'd left the hospital and all of the pieces of the past had been put together and finally laid to rest.

With the reward money they received for turning in the money from the bank robbery that their parents have been involved in, Caleb and Amelia had shared that equally with Kyle and the two men had become business partners and already had contracts to build three more houses now that their own home was finished.

Life was finally good for Amelia, and she couldn't wait for her new future to begin.

Looking out the window one more time at the snow that had made a fresh new blanket over the expanse of farmland, Amelia couldn't help but think it was the perfect day to celebrate both the New Year, and the beginning of Amelia's and Caleb's life together.

Caleb stepped behind her, and watched out the window, dipping his head into the back of her neck to steal a few kisses.

"Save that for the wedding," Kyle said jokingly as he entered the room. "I think I'll go out and help everyone get into the house safely, and leave you two love-birds alone for a minute."

Caleb gave Amelia a little squeeze. "I'm thankful that God has brought you back to me," he said. "My life would not be the same without you."

She turned around and faced him with the biggest smile he'd ever seen.

He pressed his lips to hers, unable to wait for the wedding. She indulged him for a moment, and then pulled away when the front door opened. With warm cheeks, she greeted her guests into the home that she and Caleb would begin to share this very night—just as soon as she said *I do,* and she certainly would.

THE END

You might also like:

99 cents or FREE with Kindle Unlimited

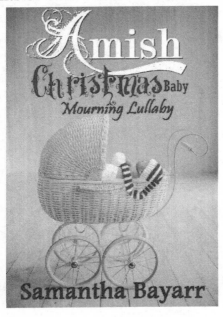

She went to apply for the nanny job. He's a rude, judgmental man....but the baby was crying. She was only there for Max. Then, like a whirlwind, in bursts the toe tappin', foot stompin', wretched Ashley, with an attitude to match. One wanted his money, the other wanted to love a deprived little boy, but there's a hiccup in the works.

Stand-Alone book. Amish Christian Romance Fiction
When Vivian answers an advertisement to spend Christmas
at a B&B in the country, she doesn't realize it is run by an
Amish family who is just as broken as she is. Trying to
rekindle the Christmas spirit, can Vivian fit in with the
Amish family and join forces to help each other through the
holidays? Will it take a modern-day miracle to make things
right again?

One tiny baby's birth, two families, two mothers, one lost &
confused, alone & tormented…The other, daughterless and
the mother of 6 rambunctious boys. Ellie always prayed for a
daughter, to teach her the Amish ways, to come alongside
her, to be her best friend and helper, but GOD had other
plans. Ellie knew GOD answers prayer and gives us the
"desires of our heart", but this one burning desire remained
unanswered……or was it?
Ellie was working on healing her broken heart until that
blessed Christmas morn. As Ellie witnesses to a young

woman, she must muster the courage and strength to do the most difficult thing she has ever done in her entire life. How can one tiny infant heal so many broken hearts? Learning to trust in the Lord, to wait patiently, is sometimes the hardest thing we can do, but wait and trust we must....GOD's timing is always the best.

Amish Daughters

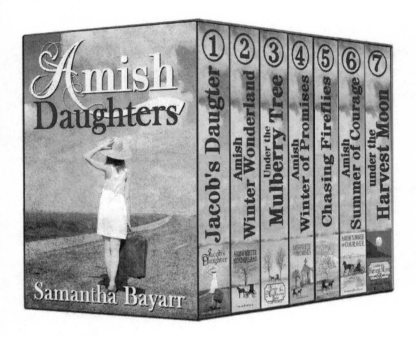

7 books in 1

Over 700 pages on Kindle or Paperback

Amish Quilters

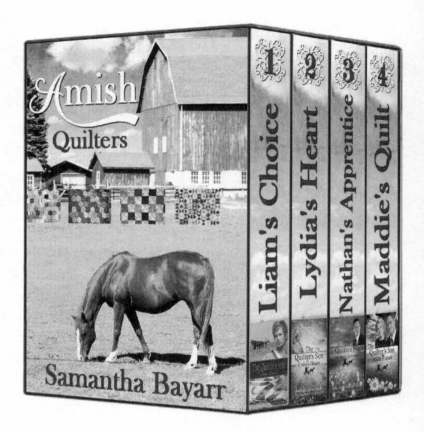

4 books in 1

Over 400 pages on Kindle or Paperback

Amish Wildflowers

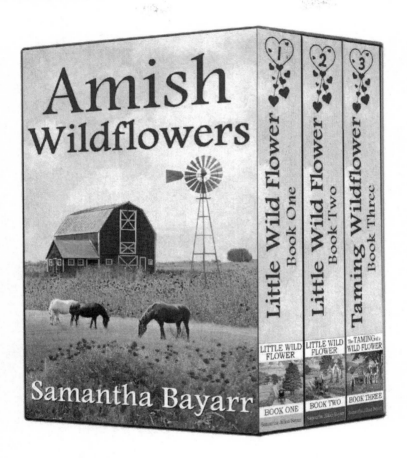

3 Books in 1

Over 500 pages on Kindle or Paperback

Western Mail Order Brides

3 Books in 1

Over 350 pages